Saving Sugarplum

Ballerinas & Billionaires: Book 1

Michelle Moras

Copyright © 2023 by Michelle Moras

All rights reserved.

No part of this publication may be reproduced, distributed, or transmitted in any form or by any means, including photocopying, recording, or other electronic or mechanical methods, without the prior written permission of the publisher, except as permitted by U.S. copyright law. For permission requests, contact michellemorasauthor@gmail.com

The story, all names, characters, and incidents portrayed in this production are fictitious. No identification with actual persons (living or deceased), places, buildings, and products is intended or should be inferred.

Book Cover by: Michelle Moras and Get Covers

Edited by: The Fiction Fix

First edition 2023

Also By Michelle Moras

The Goddess of Grace Series:
Greek Mythology Retelling Fantasy Romance Novels
Each book in the Goddesses of Grace series is a standalone novel about one of the Three Graces sisters from Greek Mythology.

Cursed by Splendor:
The untold forbidden love story of the Goddess of Splendor and the God of Fire
Available now in KU and in paperback at online retailers

Cursed by Slumber:
The untold enemies to lovers story of the Goddess of Relaxation and the God of Sleep
Coming Soon

Cursed by Sorrow:
The untold love story of the Goddess of Joy and the God of Revelry
Coming in 2024

Learn all about Michelle's books and where to get them at
www.michellemoras.com
Get exclusive giveaways, review copies, and all the latest from Michelle by subscribing to her Romance Realm newsletter:
www.michellemoras.com/pages/newsletter

Contents

Trigger Warnings		VII
Dedication		VIII
Prologue		1
1.	Curtain Call	5
2.	Overature	11
3.	The Party	15
4.	The Dance	27
5.	The March	33
6.	The Arrival	41
7.	The Magic Spell	45
8.	Battle with the Rat King	51
9.	Through the Pine Forest	57
10.	The Land of Snow	65

11.	The Enchanted Palace	71
12.	Kingdom of Sweets	75
13.	An Arabian Dance	81
14.	The Land of Chocolate	87
15.	Pas de Deux with the Prince	93
16.	Final Waltz	97
17.	Dance of the Sugarplum Fairy	103
18.	Awakening from the Dream	111
19.	Grand Finale	117
Bonus Scene		123
Acknowledgements		124
About the Author		126

Trigger Warnings

Dear Reader,

I want to forewarn you that this book contains adult themes and as a romance, has multiple sex scenes. The FMC of Saving Sugarplum experiences a brief molestation of unwanted touching. It is not done by the MC. If this topic is sensitive for you, you may not want to read this book. The last thing I want is for you to have any negative experience reading my books.

Sincerely,
Michelle

To everyone who grew up with ballerina dreams and wished you had your own Nutcracker Prince to whisk you away to magical lands and save you from your nightmares, this one's for you.

Prologue

My lips part in awe as the curtains close, the ballerina taking her final bow. The clapping and cheering of the crowd rings in my ears, and I imagine what it would be like to have them celebrating me on that stage.

"Mom, I am going to be on that stage someday," I say loudly to her over the roar of the audience.

My mother looks down at me and smiles, gently tucking my hair behind my ear. "Of course you will. You can do anything you set your heart to, darling."

I've been taking ballet lessons since I was three, but now that I'm thirteen, I've started to take it more seriously. I'm so lucky to have parents who let me pursue my dreams, though I feel guilty about how much my passion costs them. Lessons have grown more expensive now that I attend four nights a week, and that's not including the new ballet and pointe shoes. They tell me not to worry about the money, but I can't help it—I see how much they sacrifice for my dreams. I'm nervous to ask if I can audition for an intensive ballet program next summer; I don't want to make things harder on them.

All the girls at my studio are talking about where they're auditioning, and I know it would help take my training to the next level. Seeing a professional company's performance of the Nutcracker tonight makes me dream of dancing for one, something only more training can accomplish.

I chew my lip nervously as I study my mother. "Do you really think I have what it takes?" I probably ask her too much, but I don't think they would keep investing in my lessons if there wasn't a chance it could pay off.

"Of course you do! You have the same long lines and quick footwork as the dancers on that stage tonight. Most of all, when you perform, you light up the stage, just like the Sugarplum Fairy." Her fingers gently tilt my chin up to look at her. "Just keep working hard. You'll make it, I just know it."

I smile again as I nod my head. My mother always knows just what to say when I start doubting myself. Ballet is so competitive–I can't help but compare myself to the other girls. I know there will always be someone better, but I've been working my tail off in classes, and my hard work has started paying off. This year, for my studio's Nutcracker performance, I got my first role on pointe: the Mirliton dance, where we got to wear white and red striped tutus and dance with candy canes. It was so magical, and I loved every minute of our rehearsals and performances. I was so excited when Mom got tickets to see the American Ballet Company's Nutcracker in New York City for Christmas–tonight has been a dream.

"Thank you so much, Mom. Not just tonight, but for everything you do so I can keep dancing," I say, my voice low as I try not to get choked up. I've always been a quiet, sensitive girl, but it's been a bit worse since my period started this year. I was so happy to start at a typical age, since some dancers take longer from not eating enough and exercising too much. I've always been naturally lean, but I love to eat.

"You're most welcome, Clara. Your father and I will always support your dreams. We hope you never stop dancing," she says, smiling sweetly down at me. My mother grew up loving to dance as well, but she always regretted not keeping up with it after high school. I know it's one of the reasons she's willing to do whatever it takes to keep me in lessons.

We walk out of the theater and into the chilly New York night. Twinkling multi-colored lights are strung around the large Christmas tree ahead of us, and I marvel at the sounds and colors of the city at Christmastime. As we button up our peacoats to wait for a taxi to take us back to our hotel and huddle close to stay warm, I can't help the vow I make aloud.

"I promise to keep working hard so that someday, you'll get to watch me on that stage!"

"I can't wait. Merry Christmas, my little ballerina." We laugh as she bops my nose with her finger.

"Merry Christmas, Mom."

Tucked into bed later that night, I fall asleep dreaming of dancing with a Nutcracker Prince. I don't think I've ever slept so soundly.

Curtain Call

CLARA

I stand backstage, waiting for my cue to go on, butterflies of anticipation twirling in my stomach. I'm not nervous that something will go wrong, like I used to be when I was young. No, now, I'm just excited, and I know the second I step onto that stage, my performance will take over. It's the best feeling in the world, one I still pinch myself over. This really is my life. All my childhood dreams came true.

Well, almost.

I worked my way up from the corps de ballet to being a soloist for the American Ballet Company, that much closer to fulfilling my ultimate goal of being a principal. Granted, it hasn't been easy. The dance world is highly competitive, with a dark edge I wasn't expecting. Not everything is fair—roles and rank aren't always based on talent. Sometimes, it's who a dancer's family knows or how much money they donate. Then, there are those willing to sleep to the top. It's awful and I hate it, but unfortunately, it's the way things are around here.

"You ready, Clara?" my friend Gabby whispers at my side. We met at ABC's summer intensive when we were in high school, assigned randomly as roommates, and we've been best friends ever since. Our careers have been on the same trajectory: we've worked our way up together, a shoulder to lean on when I needed to cry and a friendly face when I needed a smile Gabby is one of the most gorgeous humans I've ever seen, with creamy brown skin and dark, curly hair. She has these big, bright brown eyes and incredibly long eyelashes I can't help but envy. She's making waves for being a successful black ballerina, and I couldn't be more proud to be her friend.

Tonight, we're performing together, a variation from the classical ballet *Raymonda* for the opening of our fall season. It's a classical Russian ballet based on the medieval tale of a countess torn between her love for a dashing knight and a mysterious chieftain amidst an Arab siege. Gabby and I are in the daydream pas de trois along with another dancer we both cannot stand to be around—*Emily*. While a talented dancer, Emily doesn't believe in making friends unless she thinks it'll help her work her way up. She realized early on that Gabby and I were her competition, so she didn't bother even pretending. She's just always been a bitch.

I nod my head to Gabby, my fingers twitching in anticipation. We help each other check our headpieces and make sure our pointe laces are secure. "The audience seems on fire tonight." There's nothing better than an electric crowd that gives you back as much energy as you're pouring out on stage.

"I know, I love nights like this. Have you seen Emily? She should be in place on the other side by now," Gabby asks.

"No, I haven't," I sigh, frantically looking through the sea of dancers for her familiar, platinum blonde hair. "I swear, she does this just to stress us out." I've tried so hard to be nice to Emily despite her attitude, and never once have I felt like she actually cared about anyone other than herself. Her current plan seems to be cozying up to our director, and it's working. Based on all the company gossip, no one thinks she should have gotten this role, but rumor has it, she's his new favorite pet. I try to ignore all the petty gossip, but it wouldn't surprise me if it were true.

"I'll go see if I can find her. We've got about three minutes."

Gabby nods. "Go quick, but if she's not there, don't worry about it. We can rock it without her and show Mr. Ratton she's not ready for this," she says with a smirk. I sigh; I wish it was that easy.

I run around behind the back curtain and head to the other side of the stage where Emily should be. She's not in the side wings, so I head towards the backstage door to check the stairwell. When I open it, I find Emily leaning flush against Mr. Ratton, his arm wrapped around her waist as he leans into the crook of her neck. I can't tell if he's kissing her or whispering in her ear, but their intimacy leaves me awkwardly fidgeting.

I should close the door and hope they don't see me, but it's almost time for our entrance. So, despite the fact that Emily wouldn't do the same, I take the high road and clear my throat, getting their attention.

"Emily, it's almost time," I say as sweetly as possible. Despite the annoyance I feel bubbling up in my gut, I don't want to make either of them feel awkward. I know full well it could have negative repercussions for me.

"I know, Clara, I'll be right there," she sneers, giving me a dirty look before turning back to Mr. Ratton to whisper something in his ear. He smirks, making her giggle, and I have to stop my eyes from rolling.

"Best of luck Emily, and to you too, Clara," he says with an aggravating nonchalance, as if seeing them like this is no big deal. I guess it's not, since it's his MO.

Mr. Ratton isn't a rarity in the ballet world. He was a famous principal dancer in Russia, and after retiring from dance, he became a choreographer, then a lauded director. His fame is massive, but so is his ego. Apparently, back in Russia, he was quite the playboy, and I don't think those ways have changed much. Now, he's just in a position of power, one that has dancers falling at his feet more than ever before. When you hold hundreds of careers in the palm of your hand, they're going to eat out of it. Emily seems to be licking his hand clean to get what she wants.

"Thank you, sir," I say before I turn to hurry back as fast as possible to the other side in time for my entry.

When I get back to Gabby, she looks totally panicked–we're about twenty seconds from our entrance. We both look across the stage to see Emily now in place.

"What took so long to find her?" she whispers-yells as we give our limbs one last shake.

"She was with Mr. Ratton in the stairwell," I answer quietly, not wanting anyone to overhear.

"I knew it! I knew there was something going on with them." Gabby wrinkles her nose as she shakes her head slightly. "Gross. He's so much older than her."

"He is," I agree. I hate how lecherously he looks at all of us–it makes my skin crawl whenever I feel his gaze on me. It's horrible that we have to ignore it if we don't want to risk being dropped. The only way around behavior like that is to leave the company and try your luck with another. Unfortunately, most of them have male directors with reputations just as bad—or even worse—than Mr. Ratton.

"It's time. *Merde!*" Gabby says. I have no idea why we say it, but it goes back generations, like "break a leg" in theater.

"*Merde!*" I reply before taking a deep breath to try to clear my thoughts. I can't help but keep thinking about the encounter with Emily and Mr. Ratton. There's a sour taste in my mouth–the timing of her cozying up to him oddly coincides with tonight's announcement of Nutcracker roles. As I step on stage, I force myself to focus on the music, letting go of all the negative thoughts as I pour my heart into dance.

Overature

DELANO

I'm bored out of my mind, and I could *really* use a drink.

Another performance to sit through and pretend like I care. My grandmother has dragged me to dozens of performances over the years, and the ballets are the ones I dread the most. Still, how can I deny the amazing woman who raised me?

It may be three hours of hell, but I know it's important to our company to support the arts. Plus, we do it in memory of my mother–I'll sit through to honor her, even though I don't remember her.

When I was only a year old, she and my father died on their way home from being on tour. My mother was a prima ballerina with the London Ballet, and my father was the company's CFO. It was her last tour before retiring to stay home with me.

I know it's why my grandmother has been adamant about attending these ballets my whole life. She thinks it will help me feel closer to my mother, but honestly, it's cruel torture. It just reminds me I had a mother I never knew. I've been shown every video of her dancing, and she was exquisite–I've never seen a dancer come even close to the talent my mother had. I think that's what makes me dread these things even more, why I've vowed to never date a dancer.

Regardless of my feelings, I'll suck it up and make a big donation that will maybe help me sleep a little better, hoping my mother is looking down at me proudly. I took after my father and went to work for my grandfather, helping manage his hotel in London. Since then, I've turned my grandfather's single property into a chain of luxury hotels around the world. I like to think of my efforts as a thank you for raising me, for putting up with my antics as a kid. I just want my grandparents happy and taken care of, and being a billionaire makes it that much easier.

They are the only people I love and trust in this world; I keep my inner circle small, and I'm content with that. My grandmother is always hassling me about dating and getting married, but that's the last thing I want. I'd much rather keep to one night stands and fuck buddies–it's better to break hearts than go through the pain of losing someone I care about. My friends tell me I'm a closed off bastard, but I don't see that as a bad thing. Love is painful, messy, and I can never be sure a woman doesn't just want me for my money.

My grandmother taps my arm and leans in to whisper to me.

"The next variation was one of your mother's favorites. It was one of her last roles before she was chosen as a principal dancer." I absentmindedly nod and wrap her frail hand in my own, giving it a squeeze. She loves when something reminds her of my mother.

Three dancers enter the stage in white and gold tutus with elaborate, matching headpieces. I honestly couldn't tell you what this ballet is about, and I'm about to settle in for what I'm sure will be the slowest three hours of my life when I notice the dancer in the middle.

All ballerinas are beautiful with their graceful movements and elegant costumes, but my eyes still manage to settle only on her. She seems so free up there, so bold, and I can't take my eyes off her. Every movement she makes carries so much passion–her movements seem otherworldly. Her big, brown doe eyes sparkle with mischief, and she seems so alive in each moment, but her smile is what really draws me in. There's so much joy exuding from her, and I wish I could feel an ounce of it.

I've never had this reaction to a dancer on stage before, never had one stand out so distinctly. My curiosity is piqued, and a foreign need claws up my throat–I need to know who she is.

I glance down at my program to see if I can figure out her name, but it doesn't designate who's who for this variation.

"Do you know who those dancers are?" I ask my grandmother as the variation ends and they bow to cheers of applause.

"I know two of them. The one in the middle is Clara Stahl. Everyone's talking about her becoming a principal soon," she says, and I whisper her name under my breath. *Clara.* That's my girl.

"The one to her right is Gabriella Royal. I would be shocked if she didn't get promoted next year. I'm not sure who the other is; I don't think she's been with the company long." My grandmother continues her explanation, but I've stopped listening. All I needed was her name, and I'll be damned if I don't see her later this evening.

As I roll her name around in my mind, I find myself desperate to meet her. Once I set my mind to something, nothing can hold me back–I wouldn't be as successful as I am if that wasn't the case.

"Will all the dancers be at the gala afterward?" I ask, feigning nonchalance as I keep my eyes glued to the stage.

"Of course. Has one of them caught your fancy?" she counters, a knowing smile tugging at her lips.

"Ballerinas aren't my type," I lie, the ease of which surprises even me.

"Oh, don't be ridiculous. Your mother would be offended," she says with a scoff. "Besides, how would you know? You've never dated one."

All I can do is grunt in response. She's repeated the same thing my entire life, and I've always ignored it. Thankfully, she drops it as she turns back to the performance.

As soon as the finale is over and the curtains close, I rise from my seat and excuse myself, promising to catch up with them at the gala. They give me suspicious looks, but I don't have time to explain.

I've got a ballerina to find.

The Party

CLARA

Despite being shaken up from my interaction with the director and Emily, I managed to execute my performance perfectly. Sometimes, the audience fuels my dancing to another level, and tonight was one of those nights. The audience cheered during our pirouette sequence, and I nailed the last triple. My heart races from the adrenaline as I run off stage, wiping sweat from my brow.

"That felt *so* good," Gabby squeals, grabbing my hand and giving it a tight squeeze. This variation is the most challenging because we have to be in sync the entire time, and, despite the issues with Emily, we didn't miss a beat.

"That was so much fun!" I laugh as I follow her through the wings and down the stairs to our dressing rooms. As much as I love the tutus and stage makeup, I always look forward to taking it all off. Normally, I would just change into comfortable leggings and a sweater to go home, but tonight, I have a beautiful dress to don.

The Fall Gala is one of my favorite events. Not only does it mark the start of the new season, but we get to wear our fanciest gowns. It's a star-studded event, and all the who's who of New York will be there.

Each year, we are matched with donors to sit with during dinner so we can gush about the company and help keep their donations flowing.

When I first joined the company, it made me incredibly nervous to sit with strangers and answer their questions about anything related to the company or ballet. Now, though, I actually enjoy it. The longer you're with the company, the higher your rank, the bigger donor you sit with. It's an honor of sorts, and it's a surprise every year.

When I get to my dressing room, the first thing I do is sit and take off my pointe shoes. Ballet itself may be beautiful, but it takes a toll on our feet. Luckily, I don't have too much pain from dancing en pointe, but I still cannot wait to let my feet breathe. My hands move to the bobby pins keeping my hair in place, and after what feels like an hour, I've finally pulled them all out. I wipe all the stage makeup off my face and then take a quick shower; it feels good to rinse off all the sweat. Were it any other night, I would have luxuriated, enjoying the warmth and letting my muscles relax.

Time is short, as our variation was one of the last, so after I shower, I forgo blow drying my hair and instead pull it into a low, messy bun. I like to keep my make-up simple when I'm not performing, so after applying some tinted moisturizer, adding eyeliner, mascara, and a little highlighter, I'm feeling mostly ready to go. I add a rosy lip gloss for the final touch before reaching for my dress. Long beads dangle from the black silk gown, the halter neckline accentuating my shoulders–classy and sexy. When I look in the mirror, I hardly recognize myself, the look so different from my daily leotard and tights, the dress accenting every curve of my shape.

I'm putting my heels on when I hear a knock at my door.

"Come in," I answer quickly, figuring it's Gabby to tell me to hurry up.

"Clara?" asks a deep voice, and I freeze. I know that voice, and it's the last one I expected.

I rush to the door, pulling it open to see Mr. Ratton in a tux, holding a bouquet of stunning white roses. As much of a cad as our director may be, it's easy to see how dancers fall at his feet. He's over six feet tall and looks like European royalty, with blonde hair perfectly coiffed and a long nose he uses to look down on the rest of the world. Ever since I started with the company, I've been incredibly intimidated by him.

"Mr. Ratton - I wasn't expecting you!" I say, thrown off by his presence. He's never visited me in my dressing room before.

"Excuse my intrusion, but after your performance, I wanted to deliver these flowers to you myself. You were magnificent tonight," he says as he hands me the flowers and kisses me on each cheek, as is customary in the ballet world.

My stomach flutters at his praise. I know the performance felt good, but I'm surprised to see Mr. Ratton here, figuring he would be busy making his rounds with the principal dancers or rushing off to the gala. He's never visited my dressing room before, and it feels odd to be alone with him.

"That is so kind. Thank you, sir. I really love that variation," I say shyly, biting my lower lip.

"Well, if you keep this up, you'll be seeing more roles headed your way. In fact, it seems like one of our patrons was also quite taken with your performance and has requested a last-minute change to seat you at their table."

I glance up at him, surprise widening my gaze. "That's wonderful. I'll do whatever you need."

A predatory smile curls his lips, and my gut curdles. "Whatever I need?" he asks as his demeanor shifts. He takes a step towards me, moving like a starving tiger that's just found its next meal. My heart picks up wildly, my palms starting to sweat. I've always tried to make sure I've never been alone with him, for fear of his reputation. Now, here I am, alone in my dressing room with a man I don't feel I can reject.

"For the gala, of course," I clarify, taking a small step away from him. "I look forward to this evening every year, and I know how important it is to represent the company well."

"What if I needed more than that, Clara?" he says slyly as he closes the distance between us. Only the bouquet separates our chests now, and I try to shrink back while avoiding eye contact. How do I tell him no without risking my future, the career I've worked so hard for?

"I, um, I don't know what you mean, Mr. Ratton," I stutter, feigning innocence to buy time. I really need to figure out how to get out of this situation, but all that's going through my mind is how to use those damn flowers to keep distance between us.

He reaches out a hand and trails a finger down the side of my face, making me flinch. I avert my eyes, trying to angle away from him, my entire body screaming at him to back off, but he seems to neither notice nor care.

"You are such a pretty, innocent little mouse, aren't you? You don't need to be nervous around me," he says, which is a complete lie. I've never been more nervous in my life. "I have your best interests at heart. There's so much I could teach you—I only want to help you blossom."

As he speaks, he moves his finger from my cheek, down my neck, and then traces my collarbone slowly. I hold my breath, trying my hardest not to shake. He has to know how uncomfortable I am. This is so inappropriate, and I want to scream, but I'm completely frozen.

"Mr. Ratton, I don't think you and I are talking about the same thing," I say as I raise the bouquet higher, forcing his hand off me.

His fingers wrap around the bouquet as he begins to pull it out of my hands when suddenly, my dressing room door flies open, and Gabby bursts inside. I feel myself internally sigh with relief at her intrusion.

"Clara, we're late, hurry up! It's time to... oh, Mr. Ratton, hi."

His jaw ticks as he steps away from me, turning to face Gabby. "Hello, Gabriella. I was just delivering these flowers to Miss Stahl and updating her on a slight change to her table tonight."

"Are you ready, or should I meet you there?" she asks, giving me a look with her eyebrow quirked, like she knows something's wrong.

I answer quickly before Mr. Ratton has a chance to interject.

"Stay! I was just about to leave too," I say, pleading with my eyes for her to please not leave me alone with him. I take the opportunity to grab my coat and move further out of his reach.

Thankfully, he doesn't try to follow. "I was just leaving. I have a few more...errands to run before I leave for the gala, but Clara, be sure to make an extra good impression. He is one of our top donors."

"Of course, sir," I say, avoiding his leering gaze.

"Well done tonight, both of you." He nods and then leaves swiftly, and I collapse into my chair with my head in my hands, trying to fight back tears. Sometimes, this dream job is a nightmare, and I find myself questioning if this is where I'm meant to be. I make a mental note to look into what other companies are hiring when I get home tonight. It might be time to move on, even though it grieves me to walk away from all my hard work here.

Gabby looks at me with wide eyes filled with fear. "Was he just coming onto you?" she asks. I lift my head, trying to think of the words to explain what just happened, but only tears come.

"What did he do?" Gabby asks softly. She comes closer and kneels in front of me; I'm so freaking thankful she showed up. My mind races with horrible thoughts of what would have happened if she hadn't.

"He came onto me, and I froze instead of telling him no. I don't know what to do from here, Gabby. He wants to help me "blossom". How am I supposed to tell him "no, thank you" without getting fired or demoted?"

"This isn't your fault, Clara," Gabby insists, grabbing my hand. "You weren't expecting him to show up and corner you like that." I know she's right, but I'm terrified he'll do it again. "Come on, let's fix your makeup and get going. You'll feel better once we find some champagne. Don't let him steal your night." She smiles widely at me, willing me to take some of the joy she's offering.

She's right. If I skip out, I'm just letting him win. I refuse to be his prey, to let him think he has any control over me. I may not be able to yell at him, but I can protest in quiet.

"Okay, let's do this." I dry my eyes carefully and re-apply my mascara. Following Gabby out of the theater and into the brisk, autumn night, I walk across the street to the gala venue. I hold my head high and throw my shoulders back as I enter the foyer, promising myself that I won't let Mr. Ratton ruin the joy of not only this evening, but of my future.

Next to me, Gabby gasps in delight at the gala's beauty. The theme is a magical woodland forest, and the foyer drips with crystal chandeliers and gold foliage. It's obvious no expense was spared. Gabby grabs my hand and drags me over to the champagne fountain, where we grab glasses and cheers, clinking the delicate crystals together carefully.

"To us," Gabby toasts.

"To us."

"Let's go find our tables. I'm so curious about who your mystery patron is," she says, practically dragging me down the steps into the ballroom.

"You and me both!" I've never had a donor request me before, and I'm incredibly flattered. We head over to the seating assignments, all listed on copper leaves dangling from crystals on a majestic tree. I find my name and see I'm at table three, while Gabby is unfortunately at table seven, on the other side of the room.

We part ways, promising to meet up on the dance floor after dinner. As I meander around the tables on my way to mine, I scan the room. I stop at table seven, where I sat last year, and say hello to Mrs. Bennett. A widow in her eighties, she adores the ballet and has attended this gala every year for nearly five decades. I had so much fun getting to know her last year. She sends me the sweetest notes after performances, and I just adore her. I give Mrs. Bennett a hug, chuckling with her about how I'm jealous she gets to sit at Gabby's table.

Reluctantly, I leave them behind to find my own seat. I shuffle through the ballroom, giving nods and tiny waves to the other attendees. When I finally arrive at my table, my eyes lock on the most handsome man I have ever seen.

***

Time seems to stop as we take each other in. Is this the donor who requested me? I swallow roughly, having expected some elderly gentleman, not this man who looks like he could be on the cover of GQ. His piercing gray eyes and strong jaw give him a severe look, which perfectly suits his black-on-black suit. His reddish-brown hair is slicked back on top, but it has a slight wave to it. I can see his muscles bulging under his sleeves, the fabric pulled taut against them. He practically oozes sensuality and broodiness as he sits with his leg crossed over his knee, trailing a finger around the rim of his crystal glass. He's like a modern Paul Newman, and I am nothing more than a salivating fan girl.

"Hello, you must be Clara. I'm Delano Hoffman." His voice is deep and smooth, and, to my surprise, he has a slight British accent.

"Yes, that's me. I'm Clara. It's nice to meet you, Mr. Hoffman," I stutter, cursing myself for sounding like a babbling idiot. My cheeks feel like they're on fire under his stoic gaze. Glancing around the table, I realize he's the only one seated, the other chairs empty.

"Please, call me Delano," he says, standing to pull out the chair next to him for me. "My grandfather should be back from the bar shortly."

"Is he the only other joining us this evening?" This could be a very awkward dinner with just three people. I'm not the best conversationalist, often dreading uncomfortable silence so much, I start blurting out silly jokes.

"Him and my grandmother," he says, and I can't help but wonder why they would have requested me, of all the dancers.

"How lovely for you to accompany them. I don't always see many family members at these events. You must love the ballet."

"No," he says abruptly as he takes a sip of what I assume is whiskey.

"No?" I ask, trying not to sound offended.

"No, I have never loved ballet. In fact, I have never enjoyed it." He pauses, tilting his head slightly and pinning me in place with his gaze. "Until tonight." He looks deeply into my eyes, and I'm suddenly squeezing my thighs together from the heat on his face. My stomach flutters, and I have to clear my throat to focus on the conversation.

"Do you go to the ballet often?"

"Only when I must for business purposes, such as tonight." He takes in my eager gaze, and, after a moment, he continues speaking. "My grandfather and I own a luxury hotel chain, and supporting the arts is important to him. My mother was a dancer, and I think they do it to keep her memory alive." Something vulnerable flashes in his eyes before he looks away from me and steels his expression again.

"Oh, I'm so sorry," I say softly, unsure of what else to say. I can't imagine my parents not being in my life—the thought alone has me teary-eyed.

"It's alright. My parents passed away when I was quite young." He throws back the rest of his drink quickly, as if washing away the memories. The air suddenly feels heavy between us as I try to think of what to say next.

"So, you must be quite close to your grandparents, then?"

"Yes." A man of few words, indeed. Not that I mind—super extroverted people tend to drain me—but I don't want this evening to be awkward. I really need it to be fun after the dressing room incident.

"Oh, hello, deary," a sweet, frail voice sounds behind me. His grandmother, I presume. I stand up so as to formally greet her, smoothing my hands down the front of my dress. She's an elegant woman, dressed in an emerald velvet gown. I can see the resemblance to Delano–they have the same hazel eyes and high cheekbones. She greets me with a kiss on each cheek, a gesture I return.

She introduces herself as Marie Hoffman, and her husband, Mr. Hoffman.

"Please, call me Fred. I hope our grandson hasn't been boring you," he says with a wink. Delano snorts derisively and rolls his eyes, but he gives his grandfather a slight smirk. I have yet to see him smile fully, and I find myself confusingly desperate for it.

"He's been a perfect gentleman so far," I assure him before biting my lip.

"You were stunning on stage tonight, Clara," Marie says.

"Thank you; you're too kind. It's a pleasure to meet you both," I say with a little bow. It's awfully formal, but truly a habit.

We take our seats, and Marie asks me all sorts of questions about me and my career. I tell them how I grew up in North Carolina and moved to New York at sixteen after receiving a scholarship to the company's trainee program. I've been here ever since. When Fred asks me questions about the company and our esteemed director, I have to fight the urge not to shiver at his name.

Delano remains quiet but attentive as he listens to my stories. Every time I make eye contact with him, my heart races, and I swear my cheeks heat. I've never had this reaction to anyone before, and I don't know how to handle it.

I've had a couple of boyfriends over the years—some serious, some not—but all ended eventually, for one reason or another. There were guys who didn't like my grueling schedule, guys who were just fun but not relationship material. This career really isn't conducive to a stable relationship, but I don't mind being alone. I enjoy my space and quiet time.

Still, there's just something that draws me to Delano; no one has ever left me so breathless after one, little conversation. It's overwhelming, and I can't help but wonder if he feels it too. Do I actually find him this alluring? Or is it just because my emotions are all over the place tonight?

One thing is for sure: he definitely piques my interest, and I find myself insanely curious about the mysterious man next to me.

The Dance

DELANO

I cannot take my eyes off this woman.

When I saw her on stage tonight, I knew I had to meet her. It was impulsive, out of character, but I didn't care. Before I could stop myself, I was bribing the director with donating an extra ten grand to make sure she sat at my table tonight.

I watch her while she makes conversation with my grandparents. Every few minutes, she'll work up the nerve to glance at me. I don't even think she realizes that every time our eyes meet, she licks those plump lips of hers, sweet and sensual at the same time. I shift in my chair again, trying to hide the growing bulge in my pants.

I know I should participate in their conversation more—so she's more comfortable around me—but idle small talk has never been my strong suit. I like to get to the point, and the only point I want to make is how much I'm craving this beautiful creature next to me.

The director of the ballet walks up to our table, interrupting my thoughts of being alone with just Clara.

"How are my favorite donors doing this evening?" he asks as he shakes my grandfather's hand. They exchange pleasantries, and then he moves to stand directly behind Clara's seat. My body tenses as I watch him run his knuckles down the back of her neck before placing his hand on her shoulder. At first, I assume they must be together–why would he touch her like that if they weren't? But then, her entire body stiffens, her features morphing into panicked unease, and I start to fume.

"And how are you enjoying the company of our lovely Clara?" he asks, looking pointedly down his nose at me. My jaw clenches as I think about all the ways I could destroy this man. Men in roles of power thinking they can touch a woman without their consent doesn't fly with me, and it's clear Clara isn't comfortable around him as he keeps rubbing her shoulder with his thumb.

"She's just as captivating in person as she was on stage," I drawl, looking deep into her eyes before glancing back up at Mr. Ratton, injecting venom into my stare.

"Yes, she really is something. She has a bright future with our company. We were just discussing her career goals earlier this evening, isn't that right, my darling?" he asks her.

She doesn't even turn her head to speak to him. Instead, I watch her bristle before nodding in response. Something isn't right, and I'm going to get to the bottom of it. I push back my chair and hold out my hand to her as I stand. "Clara, would you do me the honor of dancing with me?"

"Oh, of course. I..." she starts to answer as she places her hand in mine. I give her what I hope is a reassuring squeeze as she stands, but then the dimwit has the audacity to interrupt.

"Actually, I was hoping to borrow Clara for a moment. Would you mind if you held off on that dance a little longer?"

"Actually, I do mind," I growl as I pull Clara closer and wrap my arm around her waist. The hold is purely possessive, surprising even myself. I look down at Clara, making sure she's not uncomfortable with my contact. Her body immediately relaxes under my touch, and something warm flickers inside me in response.

"Surely business can wait until tomorrow, Mr. Ratton. This evening is supposed to be for your company to celebrate and enjoy."

His eyes widen for the briefest of moments before he schools his expression into a tight smile. He's obviously a man used to getting his way. He may be used to having power here, but I am more than willing to show him he shouldn't mess with me.

"Of course. I wouldn't want to ruin anyone's evening," he says with a fake smile plastered across his face. He bids my grandparents farewell and walks away, and I let out an internal sigh of relief that he didn't push me further.

"Are you okay?" I whisper into Clara's ear as I guide us towards the dance floor.

"What do you mean?" she asks, as if she thinks I missed Ratton's entire show.

I don't answer as I pull her body flush against mine, wrapping an arm around her waist and intwerwining our fingers. Our bodies sway effortlessly to the music, moving in tandem like it was always meant to be this way. Goosebumps dot her arms, and a beautiful flush stains her cheeks. I'm not sure if it's from embarrassment or if she just likes being in my arms, but I hope it's the latter.

"Look at me," I say in a gentle whisper.

She slowly turns her beautiful face back to mine, my heart beating wildly as our eyes meet. Her eyes are welling up with tears, but she's looking up at me like I'm her hero, and fuck, if that doesn't make me hold her tighter. The urge to take her away from here and never let her go is overwhelming. I'm not used to feeling like this, and I feel like I'm losing my mind.

"I know you were uncomfortable back there," I tell her, spinning us across the dance floor. Her pulse quickens, the beat visible under the delicate skin of her neck. "I didn't like the way he was touching you," I rumble.

"I honestly don't know what to say, except thank you for saving me from whatever that was," she whispers, looking away from me.

I lightly grab her chin, bringing her face back to mine. Her skin is so soft, everything about her so delicately beautiful. "Never apologize for someone else's mistakes," I command, relishing in the way she smiles at me. "Is he a problem I can help you fix?" I hope she says yes, because after what I saw, I'd happily have him removed. I know we're one of their biggest donors, and my voice will have a bigger impact.

"I can handle it. Unfortunately, it's just a part of this world," she says with a shrug.

The casualness with which she speaks makes my blood boil. I've heard rumors of this sort of thing in ballet companies; there was a big scandal a few years back in a different company, where dancers broke their silence about some famous choreographer that had been molesting them for years. If that's what's happening here, I'll be damned if I don't get to the bottom of it.

"I wouldn't want to make a big fuss and then jeopardize my career over a little shoulder rub." She chuckles, the sound forced. I may not be the most forthcoming man with my own emotions, but I find reading others easy, and right now, she's clearly hiding her feelings, probably for fear of embarrassment.

"I have no doubt you can handle it, but you shouldn't have to. Nothing about what you just said is acceptable, but I trust you would turn him in if he crossed any lines, yes?" When she doesn't answer and instead bites her lower lip, I push a little harder. "Promise me."

"Of course," she says timidly, but I don't think either of us are convinced.

"Good."

We keep dancing for the remainder of the song in agreeable silence. She feels perfect in my arms, and with every note, we somehow move closer. I've never felt so comfortable with someone so quickly, and with the way she melts into me, I'm left to assume she feels the same. The top of her head rests just under my jaw, and I can't help my subtle intake of breath. She smells like something floral—roses, I realize—but there's a hint of something sweet as well, like vanilla. She pulls back and gives me a shy smile.

"Want to grab a drink and go somewhere a little quieter? We can talk and get to know each other better," I ask. Her light brown eyes sparkle, and as I await her answer, I can't help but notice how pretty her lips are, just begging to be kissed.

"That sounds perfect."

With my hand on the small of her back, I guide us off the dance floor, weaving through the tables towards the bar. As we walk, people turn and look at us, some more subtle than others. I don't blame them, as I can't take my eyes off this stunning woman either. I'm damn lucky she's even giving me the time of day. For the first time in a long time, I want to open up.

The March

CLARA

Someone pinch me–this man cannot be real.

The way Delano stood up to Mark and then whisked me away to the dance floor made me feel so safe and protected. I've never dated anyone who oozes so much strength and confidence but is so kind and honest at the same time. He's as intriguing as he is handsome, and I don't want this night to end.

He guides me towards the bar, his hand warm and firm on the small of my back. The touch gives me goosebumps, causing my pulse to race. When we get to the bar, I grab a flute of champagne while he orders an expensive sounding whiskey on the rocks.

"Cheers to you, Clara," he says, a smirk pulling at his firm lips. I could get lost in the intensity of his eyes, in the way they draw me closer. It doesn't hurt that the deep tenor of his voice is pure sin.

"Why cheers to me?" I ask, quirking a brow in question.

He pauses, head canting to the side. "Because I am very happy to have met you tonight."

"Well, I guess I can cheers to that," I say with a wink as we clink our glasses. We sip our drinks and gaze out at the crowd; the gala is in full swing, and it's turning into quite the party, with the music and chatter growing louder by the minute.

"Would you like to go somewhere a little quieter?" he asks, his eyes scanning the ballroom.

"Sure; I know just the spot." I grab his hand and lead him out onto the balcony. There's a few other people out here enjoying the lovely, crisp fall evening, but it's much quieter than inside.

"Your grandparents won't mind that we left them alone?" I ask, feeling a bit guilty.

"No," he says, taking a sip of whiskey. "Honestly, they're probably glad to have time to mingle without my glares scaring people off."

I laugh, shaking my head as I turn to face him fully. "Oh, I doubt that. I can tell how much they love you, broody personality and all," I say teasingly, elbowing his side. That earns me the first full smile I've seen, and I have to bite back a gasp. He is the most attractive man I have ever seen. What in the world does he want with me?

"So, was ballet what you always wanted to pursue?" he asks, leaning his elbows on the railing. He seems genuinely interested, and for the first time in a while, I find myself *wanting* to open up. It's been a few years since my last relationship, and I had sworn off men for a while to focus on my career. I mirror his movements, looking out over the gardens below.

"Always. When I was a teenager, my mom took me to see the Nutcracker. I knew the moment I saw the Sugarplum Fairy that I would be on the stage someday." My eyes get lost in the memory for a moment, and when he doesn't respond right away, I worry that perhaps the story was too cheesy. When I look over to him, though, he flashes me a sweet smile, tampering any of the nerves I feel.

"And do you love it as much as you thought you would?"

"Hmm, that's hard to say," I answer. "When I'm on stage, definitely. That is where I am happiest. I love class, too." I smile, thinking of all the hard work it's taken to get to where I am. "But the competitiveness and politics of the job aren't fun," I add with a grimace. I don't really want the conversation to circle back around to Mark, so I ask him a question before he can ask another.

"What about you? Do you like your job? Working with your family?"

"I do. I love continuing what my grandfather started and expanding on it. I get to travel all over the world and see new places," he answers, and I can tell he takes great pride in his work. I can't help but think about how different our lives are, and I briefly wonder if we could make a relationship work. I shake my head at the ridiculous thought. I just met the man. I can't possibly fall for him this fast. It's probably the champagne.

"Do you like to travel?" he asks.

I nod. "Yes, definitely. I wish I could travel more; there are so many places I want to see and experience. One of my favorite things about this company is the chance to go on tour or be a guest artist at other companies, but I haven't gotten the opportunity yet."

He inclines his head. "Have you ever been to London?"

"I haven't, but I would love to someday," I say wistfully.

"Well, we will have to change that, won't we?" he asks as he steps closer. "I think I would enjoy being your tour guide." He gently reaches his arm around me, resting his hands on the railing on either side of my hips. I'm suddenly engulfed by the warmth of his body, and I can't help but lean back into him, savoring this moment. Being close to him is so different from Mark's advances. Whereas Mark made me feel threatened, Delano makes me feel safe.

"I'd like that," I say softly. My throat feels tight as I try to swallow, my tongue darting out to wet my lips. I take a deep breath and try to tamp down the butterflies exploding in my stomach as I turn my head to look up at him. When we lock eyes, I realize I want him to kiss me.

"Good," he breathes as he leans closer. My breath catches—it's happening. This insanely gorgeous man is going to kiss me. I can feel his breath tickle my face as he gently grabs my cheek with one hand and holds the back of my neck with the other.

"May I kiss you?" he whispers, eyes darting to my lips and back up again. Instead of answering, I stand on the tips of my toes and brush my lips against his. He groans into the kiss and deepens it, pulling my bottom lip between his teeth. It sends a zap of warmth down to my core, and I can't help but reach up to pull his face closer to mine. He swipes the seam of my lips with his tongue, and I open up for him as we tangle our tongues together. My hands slide up into his hair as I get lost in the feel of his mouth on mine.

A familiar voice clearing their throat causes us to pull apart, chests heaving, staring at each other like we just found lost treasure. That was the best kiss of my life.

"Sorry to interrupt, but Mr. Ratton is about to make the announcement about the winter season, and I didn't think you would want to miss it," Gabby explains, giving me a knowing smile. As sad as I am that our kiss can't continue, she's right. We've been speculating for months about the principal Nutcracker roles, and I wonder if this will be my year.

I give Delano an apologetic smile, and he grabs my hand, giving it a reassuring squeeze. We follow Gabby back inside and find our seats next to his grandparents. Delano pulls out my chair for me before taking the seat next to me, and his grandmother looks at us with bright eyes as Delano kisses my temple.

A loud clinking of glass grabs everyone's attention as Mr. Ratton takes the stage at the front of the ballroom. Someone hands him a microphone, and the entire room goes quiet.

"Thank you for joining us this evening to celebrate our fall season. I want to thank our tremendous donors for their support and for helping keep the arts thriving in our city." He pauses to let the attendees clap, and my heartbeat picks up. "This is always a special time of year as we celebrate our dancers' achievements and look forward to our transition into our winter repertoire. We have a mix of both modern and classical ballets planned for the winter season. Our beloved Nutcracker will again be the diamond of our performances, and some of our dancers will be guest principals for other companies." Another round of applause sounds as Mark waits until the clapping dies down.

"Now, the moment our dancers have been waiting for: the lead Nutcracker roles. If I call your name, please stand. Darcy Russell and Alexander Pavlova will assume the roles of Sugarplum Fairy and her Cavalier. Emily Smith and Joshua Foster will perform as the Snow Queen and King, while Gabriella Adams will perform the Dew Drop Fairy."

Everyone claps politely, and I can't help but feel my heart sink that I wasn't one of the names called. I thought for sure Gabby or I would at least get Snow Queen, but it looks like Emily's *relationship* with Mark gave her the edge. I try to not show my disappointment as I search for Gabby in the crowd. She's looking right at me, giving me a big, dramatic eye roll. The gesture makes me smile despite the tears threatening to spill. I clap in her direction, hoping she can see how happy I am that she got Dew Drop, even though we both know she deserves more.

Delano must sense my frustration, because he sets his hand on my thigh under the table. I glance back at him and smile. He gives my thigh a squeeze in response, and my thoughts immediately go back to our kiss as a blush blooms across my cheeks..

Mark continues his speech with announcements for those doing guest performances. At this point, I'm not holding my breath, assuming I'll have the same role as last year. I silently convince myself to be happy with what I have.

"And now, the guest principal roles. Those chosen will be headed to England, dancing with the London Ballet. The role of Sugarplum Fairy and her Cavalier will go to Clara Stahl and Trevor Reed. Snow Queen and King will be Amelie Jones and Marcus Mitchell, and Dew Drop goes to Tiffany Jones."

I feel like all the air has been punched from my lungs. I can't believe it! I'm finally getting my dream role.

Delano whispers in my ear. "Stand up, beautiful." I was so shocked by the news, I was frozen in my seat. I quickly stand, feeling supremely awkward with everyone staring at me. I once again look for Gabby, only to find her standing with a beaming smile, giving me a quick thumbs up.

I sit back down as Mr. Ratton continues his speech, but I'm no longer listening.

"Looks like you'll be going to London sooner than later," Delano says with a smirk.

"I can't believe it. This is surreal. I'm so excited!" I'm smiling so hard, I think my cheeks are about to split.

"You deserve it," he says, and I melt once again under his praise. "I just hope you'll have enough time in your busy schedule for me to show you around."

"I'll make time," I promise with a blush.

"I'm glad, but I don't think I can wait until then to see you again," he says.

My stomach flutters harder. "How long are you in New York?" I ask.

"I was hoping you'd ask," he says and my heart stutters knowing he wants more time with me.

Can this night get any better? Somehow, I've landed my dream role and met my dream man, all in the last hour. Tonight might have started as a nightmare, but now, I feel like I'm living in a dream.

The Arrival

DELANO

"How long are you in New York?" she asks.

"I was hoping you'd ask," I say. I'm willing to change all my flights and plans to stay longer, to keep getting to know her. I've never craved someone like this. There's just something so intriguing about her.

That she'll be over on my side of the pond soon seems like fate. The prospect of spending time with her, delving into conversations beyond the superficial, fills me with a sense of anticipation I haven't felt in a long while.

"Meet me tomorrow," I suggest, and I can't help but smile at the blush that creeps along her cheeks. She's so fucking beautiful, she makes my heart practically split with how hard it pounds, and I fight the urge to kiss her right here, right now.

"I have rehearsals later in the day, but I'm free in the morning," she answers shyly. I wonder how many men she's dated, because she seems so timid. I'm used to women boldly throwing themselves at me, but everything about Clara, from the way she smiles to the way she talks, is demure and gentle. It's so attractive, and I'm shocked she's still single. All I can think about is making her mine.

"Just name the time and place, and I'll be there," I say, handing her my phone. "Put your number in."

We exchange numbers, and, with a shared smile, I lean in to kiss her on the cheek. When I get a whiff of her scent, I can't help but inhale deeply. She smells like vanilla and sandalwood, and it's absolutely *intoxicating*. Her breath hitches as I linger; when I pull back, our eyes lock, filling with unspoken desire.

When I get back to my hotel room that night, I can't help but wonder if the deep loneliness I usually feel coming home to an empty room might not be the case much longer. Just as I turn off the light and lay my head on the pillow, my phone dings. I pick it up, the light so bright in the dark that I have to squint. It's from Clara, and my heart hammers in my chest, hoping she's not already backing out.

> *I got us a reservation at my favorite breakfast place, French Toast, for 10am. See you there. Sweet dreams. XOXO, Clara*

The way this girl makes me smile is the craziest thing. I reply instantly, not wanting to keep her awake or wondering.

Morning can't come soon enough. In the meantime, I'll be dreaming of the beautiful ballerina I met tonight - Delano

I know I sound corny, and that's not usually my style, but I can't help it. It's like she brings out this whole other side I didn't know I had. There's something special about her, and I intend to discover all I can.

***

I could barely sleep, up at 5am, staring at the ceiling. I had the most bizarre dreams about Clara and her director. In my dream, his face morphed into a huge rat head, and I had to fight him in a duel at dawn to protect her. My instincts are never wrong about people, and I know my dream was my subconscious warning me. He reminds me of a rat, and his name is Ratton, so the shoe fits.

After working out, showering, and getting coffee, I decide to head out early so I can scope out where we're meeting. The restaurant is on the Upper West Side, so I leave my hotel and meander through Central Park. It's a beautiful morning, with clear skies and a crisp autumn breeze blowing gently through the trees. Autumn in New York is picture perfect, and for a moment, I let myself imagine what it would be like to live here, with Clara.

A couple walks by, pushing a baby stroller and walking their dog, and for the first time, I feel a pang in my chest at the sight. I want that someday. I shake my head at these insane thoughts–I'm getting way too far ahead of myself.

The walk takes longer than I expected, and by the time I get to French Toast, it's twenty minutes to ten, so I decide to check in and wait for her at our table. It's a little corner place and very classically French, with red and white striped awnings and old photos of Paris on the walls. Paris isn't one of my favorite cities, but I'd love to take Clara there. I wonder if she's ever hoped to dance at the Paris Opera House. Another thing to ask eventually.

The little bell on the door jingles, and my breath catches in my throat as I see Clara walk through. She's dressed casually in tight black jeans and a creamy knit sweater, and I can't believe that she somehow looks just as stunning dressed down as she did dressed up last night. Her golden-brown hair cascades down her back, and I decide I really like her hair down. At this point, though, I don't think there's a version of her I wouldn't like.

I watch as she checks in with the hostess and they point her in my direction. As soon as she turns her head, our eyes lock, and I can't fight back the smile that crosses my face. She gives me a shy smirk, and once again, I notice the blush that floods her cheeks.

I wonder what other places I can make blush for me.

The Magic Spell

CLARA

I am so out of my league.

His smirk melts me. He is confidence personified, and as he stands to greet me, I have to will my nerves to calm down. Dancing in front of thousands of people doesn't make my stomach flip, but this?

I spent the entire morning trying to convince myself this is just a crazy little fling that I need to get out of my system, but everytime we lock eyes, it's like time stops. My brain is telling my heart that it's just chemistry–*really strong chemistry*–and since I haven't been with anyone in awhile, I'm going to let myself enjoy him. It's only for today, anyway. Maybe I'll see him once or twice in London, but it'll end there. I'll get whatever this is out of my system, and then it's back to focusing on ballet.

I slowly take him in as I sit down.

He's wearing a black turtleneck that shows off his toned biceps and dark blue jeans wrapped around strong thighs. I've never seen a man so achingly beautiful. I think part of what draws me to him is the dark, tortured soul vibe he's got going on, and I am here for it.

"Good morning, beautiful," he says in a deep voice that sends tingles through my body. He leans in and kisses my cheek, and I kiss his in return. How it feels like I've known him my whole life when it's been mere hours is beyond me. He intimidates me but comforts me at the same time. I hate to say it, but this connection is magical. I could barely sleep last night thinking about him.

"Good morning," I say as I take my seat. He holds it out for me before sitting across from me at our little table. God, he's the perfect gentleman, too. Here in New York, this sort of chivalry is ancient history. None of my dates have ever pulled my chair out, let alone stand to greet me. Maybe this is all a dream, but if it is, I really don't want to wake up.

"How are you?" I ask.

"Better now," he says, flashing me a broad smile and giving me a glimpse of his dimples. *I'm a sucker for dimples.* "How did you sleep?"

I probably shouldn't tell him that I dreamt of him all night–that would be embarrassing. "Fine. I was pretty exhausted, but I still had a hard time falling asleep," I explain before I quickly change the subject. "Did you find this place okay? I wasn't sure how familiar you are with New York."

"I couldn't sleep either," he says with a wink, "which is why I got here early. That, and I wanted to make sure I found it, which was no problem," he says.

SAVING SUGARPLUM

The waiter, a grouchy old man, comes over and takes our order. I order the croque monsieur, along with a mimosa–I could use a little liquid courage right now. Delano orders an omelet, and then we fall into conversation that flows easily. We exchange stories about our childhoods and our current careers, and I'm fascinated by Delano's ambitions and tales of opening new hotels in foreign places.

"I've never been to Europe, but I'd love to see it all someday. It sounds like a fairytale," I say.

"Well, I'm more than happy to show you. Do you know when you'll leave for London?" he asks.

"I imagine I'll rehearse here through November and fly to London just before the performances. That'll give us enough time to rehearse with the company a couple times before the first performance. Have you seen the London Ballet's Nutcracker?"

He dabs his mouth with his napkin, and I have to force myself to not stare at those perfect lips of his, remembering how they felt against my own.

"Yes, many times. It's where my mother was a principal. It's a tradition for my grandmother and I to go. I imagine I'll be buying us tickets for multiple performances this year," he says, flashing me a smile.

"And why might that be?" I ask, my mouth quirking up to one side. I'm sure I already know the answer, but I'm dying to hear him say it.

He pushes his plate to the side, leaning over the table on his elbows and crooking his index finger in a "come here" gesture. I comply and lean in, our noses practically touching. My hair falls forward, cascading around us like a curtain, and he gently pushes one side behind my shoulder as he leans in closer to whisper in my ear.

"You see, there's this ballerina I can't stop thinking about, and I just want more. More time, more moments, more of everything with her. So, I'll buy all the tickets, because I would do anything for a mere glimpse of her on stage." Then, as if that didn't already have me in a puddle, he moves his lips lower and kisses my neck slowly. A soft moan escapes me, and for a moment, I forget that we're in the middle of a restaurant. Delano pulls away and sits back against his chair, while I sit there, frozen in bliss.

"Want to get out of here?" he asks with a knowing look, and I look at my phone to check the time.

"Shit. I have class in thirty minutes," I say, cringing when Delano's smirk drops.

"I have to fly out tonight, but I'll do anything to spend more time with you before I leave. Can I walk you to the studio and then meet you after?" he asks.

I take a deep breath to steady my racing heart before answering. "You can definitely walk me back, but I have rehearsals the rest of the day, I'm afraid."

"Well, it looks like I'll be pulling my donor card and watching rehearsals today," he says, that smirk returning. "If that's okay with you, of course," he adds hopefully. My jaw drops open slightly, shocked that he seems as desperate as I am to see him again.

"You really don't need to do that. I'm sure you have much more important things to do," I say, even though I'd love nothing more.

Delano reaches forward again and cups my cheek. God, his hands are big, and I can't help but lean into his palm. Distantly, I wonder what they might feel like on the rest of my body.

He lowers his voice to a deep whisper. "Look, Clara, I don't want to come on too strong, but I have to be honest. I have never been this captivated by someone in my entire life. You have enchanted me, and I will do anything to stay caught in your spell. Tell me you feel this too. Tell me I'm not alone here," he pleads, and the groveling in his voice gives me goosebumps.

"I feel it too," I whisper. "It's crazy, and I don't know what's happening, but," I swallow, holding his gaze, "I don't want it to end." I've never had a man be this honest and up front with me before, but when I think of the other guys I've dated, I realize maybe they were just boys, and Delano is the first real man I've experienced.

Then he kisses me, and I come undone. The kiss is deep and sensual as we lose ourselves in the moment. I suck his bottom lip between my teeth just as he did to mine earlier, eliciting a deep moan from his chest, barely audible over the chattering in the restaurant. When we pull apart, our chests heave in sync.

"Let's go," he whispers, and I take his hand as I follow him out of the restaurant and into the crisp day.

As we walk down the busy streets hand in hand, I can't help but feel like my heart is going to burst. This all feels too good to be true, a fact I'm reminded of when I remember he's leaving.

Battle with the Rat King

DELANO

As I sit in the sun-drenched studio, watching Clara gracefully move across the floor, my heart swells with pride and admiration. Every delicate step, every elegant turn, speaks volumes about her talent and dedication. I am captivated by her presence, lost in the beauty she brings to life with her body.

I can't help but imagine what that body would feel like underneath and on top of me. I try to block out those thoughts, but it's impossible to watch her and not have my cock stirring to life in my trousers. I love how the leotard and tights she wears shows off her hourglass figure, and yet I hate that others get to see her like this everyday. Jealousy flares inside me, the ugly emotion one I'm not familiar with.

My eyes narrow as I observe Mark, the ballet director, use Clara for a demonstration in the middle of the room. All of Clara's muscles tense as he grabs her by the waist and lifts her into the air. Once he has her fully lifted, he releases one arm and moves it underneath her thigh as she changes her leg position. I've seen this pas de deux a hundred times, but never have I seen the partner's hand move fully to the ballerina's crotch, pushing his thumb into the bottom of her leotard between her legs. Then, he looks at me through the glass doors and smirks.

My vision goes red. His lingering touch, the lecherous glint in his eyes—it ignites a fury within me that I cannot contain. I look at Clara, her face pale as he sets her down while the rest of the dancers applaud. She's obviously shaken, and no one seems to notice or care–they're too caught up in learning the choreography. Meanwhile, Mark attempts to carry on rehearsal as if he didn't just violate one of his dancers.

I swiftly enter the studio, my steps purposeful and determined as I make my way towards Mark, now standing at the front of the room. Clara stands off to the side stretching, and her eyes go wide when she sees me. The intensity of my gaze bores into him as I corner him, my voice low but laced with a mixture of anger and warning.

"Mark, a word?" I seethe, my tone low and menacing. He nods and follows me out to the foyer, clearly loath to upset his biggest donor. Once we're alone, I step into his personal space.

"If I ever see or hear of you making any advances towards Clara again, I will ensure that you regret it. I won't hesitate to pull all my funding and more if you continue to take advantage of your dancers."

Mark's face contorts with a mix of surprise and fear, the realization that he got caught striking him like a lightning bolt. His words stumble out, filled with nervousness and attempts at justification that I don't let take root.

"Your position of authority does not grant you the right to take advantage of the dancers under your charge," I continue, my voice steady and unwavering. "Clara is a talented artist, and she deserves to work in an environment free from harassment. So, here's how this is going to go. After rehearsal today, you are going to make the necessary arrangements for Clara and her partner to head to England *tonight* to start rehearsing with the London Ballet. Understood?"

Mark stares at me with wide eyes, his body tense as the silence stretches between us.

"Is that understood?" I press again.

"Fine," is all Mark says. The asshole knows he's screwed with no way out.

"Good. And Mark? Cross that line again, and you will face even worse consequences," I growl as I sit back down. I briefly make eye contact with Clara through the glass doors as he walks back into the studio, and I give her a small nod. There's no way in hell I'll leave Clara alone with this rodent again.

Their rehearsal wraps up thirty minutes later, and Clara makes her way to me, her eyes filled with a mix of confusion and concern.

"Delano, what did you say to Mr Ratton?" she asks, her voice tinged with worry. "He just announced to the entire class that my partner and I leave for London *tonight*." I take her hands in mine, feeling the tremor running through her delicate fingers. With a deep breath, I speak, my words laced with protectiveness.

"Clara, I saw Mark touch you during that lift," I explain, my voice gentle, not wanting her to feel any shame. "I couldn't stand idly by while he accosted you. I made it clear that his actions would not be tolerated." Tears well in Clara's eyes, a mixture of gratitude and vulnerability shining through her beautiful features. She wraps her arms around me, and I do the same, loving the feel of her head against my chest.

"Thank you, Delano," she whispers, her voice filled with emotion. "Thank you for standing up for me, for protecting me. He's never done that before, but I fear the further I move up, the more he thinks he can have his way whenever he wants," she says with a shaky voice.

The thought of him doing this to all the dancers makes me ill. I may not have told him, but I definitely plan to report him to the board of directors.

"You don't need to worry about him anymore, okay?" I say as I take her chin in my palm. "I'm going to do everything in my power to shield you and the other dancers from any further harm."

"I don't deserve you," she says as she stands on her tiptoes to kiss me, a tender kiss that ends too soon.

"Never say that, Clara. You deserve the world, and I want to be the person who gives it to you." I will be a force that shields her from harm, her unwavering support in a career that can sometimes be cruel.

"So I guess we don't have to say goodbye today after all," she says with a sweet smile that I want to commit to memory forever. "Maybe we can meet up at the airport?"

"I can do better than that. Let's go get you packed up, and I'll make sure you get on my flight. We'll go together. How does that sound?" I don't tell her that my flight happens to be my own personal plane. That can be a surprise for later.

"This is all happening so fast. I'm not sure what I'm supposed to do," she says, twisting her fingers in her hands.

"Look, I know we just met, but I think we were supposed to cross paths. I'd really love to help you get to know London, and maybe we could get to know each other more in the process. Let me help you," I plead, practically begging her at this point.

She's silent for a moment, looking off to the side, but when she turns back to face me, she smiles. "This is insane, but okay. I'm happy to have your help, and if I'm honest, I'm so happy to not have to say goodbye," she says, her cheeks turning a lovely shade of red.

We walk hand in hand down the stairs and out into the crisp night. I can't wait to get her to London and show her my home. I'm not sure if her feelings for me are as deep as mine are for her, but I intend to use our time together to convince her she belongs with me.

Through the Pine Forest

CLARA

By the time we got to my apartment, I had stopped shaking after being violated by Mark. Not only did he majorly cross a line, but I was mortified that he did it in front of the entire company. I'm not sure what was worse: him touching me, or that no one blinked an eye. Well, no one but Delano, that is.

God, just when I thought this man can't get anymore perfect, he came barging in like a knight in shining armor to save me. When I saw the stern look on his face and his clenched fists, I thought he was going to punch Mr. Ratton. As shocked and embarrassed as I was, it was so hot seeing him put Mark in his place. Delano radiates this calm power that I am attracted to like a drug, and he makes Mark look pathetic in comparison.

I've never been more thankful for having met him than at that moment.

As I pack a duffel full of all my ballet clothes and pointe shoes and a roller for everything else, Delano is on his phone booking my plane ticket. His back is to me as he looks out the window to the city below, and I take a moment to appreciate the view. I've never been with a man so devastatingly handsome. I admire his firm backside and broad shoulders, loving how his dark reddish hair slightly curls in the back. I can't wait to kiss him again so I can run my hand through it.

My phone ringing pulling me out of my lustful haze. Gabby's face lights up my screen, and I answer it immediately.

"Oh my god! Are you okay? What's happening? I got out of my rehearsal and everyone's flustered and whispering about you," she spits out, talking almost faster than I can comprehend.

"I'm so sorry! I didn't have a chance to find you before I left. I'm okay, better now. Mark fingered me through my leotard during a lift demonstration and Delano saw it happen. He threatened Mark, and now I'm off to London immediately."

"Okay, that's hot. Thank goodness he was there!" Gabby says, and I couldn't agree more. "I'm going to miss you, though."

I sigh. "I know. I'm not sure what I would've done if Delano hadn't stepped in. I was so freaked out. I'll miss you too, but I'll be back before New Years, and we will ring in another year together!"

"Well, I hope it goes fast. I can't believe I have to survive a Nutcracker season without you," she says, and my heart sinks at the thought. We've always had each other through the craziness of sixteen performances.

"I know; it won't be the same," I say.

"True, but I have a feeling that this might be your best season. You're getting whisked away to the real Land of Snow by a gorgeous billionaire. You're living the dream, girl!" she says, and I can't help but smile. She's right–this is unreal.

I end our conversation to find Delano is off his phone as well, those alluring eyes watching me.

"Who was that?" he asks, titling his head to look at me inquisitively.

"Oh, just my friend Gabby. She heard about the issue with Mark and wanted to check in," I say as Delano comes to stand in front of me. I can't help but inhale his scent every time he's close. He smells like pine trees and whiskey with a hint of leather, and I can't get enough. I'm sure he wears some super expensive cologne–whatever it is, I need it bottled up.

"I like the way she made you smile. She must be a good friend," he says. "I hope I can make you smile like that soon."

"You already do," I say with a big smile. I place my hands on his chest, tilting my head back to look up at him. I love how tall he is.

"Good, because I want all your smiles. I want you to feel safe enough to give me all of you," he says as he caresses my neck with the backs of his fingers, sending chills down my spine. A fire I've never felt before ignites within me, and I just want more.

"Delano," I whisper, not sure how to tell him I'm already his.

"What do you want, beautiful? We have about thirty minutes before we need to leave." He kisses up my neck and then whispers in my ear. "Tell me what you need." I'm so turned on, I can barely talk. I've never been one to tell a guy what I wanted or needed, and the thought makes me blush.

"I need you. All of you," I say, hoping he understands.

"I'll give you whatever you want," he says in a deep voice, cupping my face. "I will make you feel so good, but if at any point it's too much, tell me, and I'll slow down." I love how sweet and careful he is with me, but right now, I don't need sweet. I want him to ruin me.

"I want this. No need to go slow," I say, smiling at him, and he groans before slamming his lips to mine.

We get lost in feverish kisses, our hands roaming each other's bodies. Everywhere he touches me feels like it's on fire. Our clothing slowly comes off, piece by piece, between kisses and caresses. Something about him slowly rolling down my tights has me squirming with desire. I pull him down onto the bed, and he braces himself on top of me, his corded arms landing on either side of my head. He kisses me languidly before he stands, and I whine at the loss of his touch.

"You are the most stunningly gorgeous thing I've ever laid eyes on," he says as he slowly soaks my nakedness in.

"You aren't so bad yourself," I breathe as I take in how sexy he looks with his disheveled hair.

"Scoot back," he instructs and I happily obey. I can't help but giggle as he licks his lips watching me shift on the bed. I've never been so on display before. I thought I'd be embarrassed, but the way he looks at me just makes me feel more confident.

Delano gets on the bed, perched on his knees in front of me. "Spread your legs for me, baby. Let me see every inch of you," he purrs. I slowly open my knees, stretching into the splits, earning another groan from him. "Can I taste you?" he asks with eager eyes.

I nod, a little nervous—no other guy has ever been able to make me come like that, and I don't want to disappoint him.

He leans down and kisses the inside of my knee, then proceeds to lick his way up my leg in one swoop, all the way to my core. He kisses my glistening lips while watching as I squirm with anticipation. I'm already feeling so sensitive, tingling everywhere his lips touch. When he licks up the middle to my clit, I feel like I'm going to burst already. I toss my head back and arch my back, trying to manage the intensity of the pleasure rolling through me. He works my clit with his incredible tongue before delving a finger into my core as I gasp.

I can't get enough of the groans and noises he's making, like he's devouring the most delicious meal he's ever had. I'm lost in pleasure, squirming before him. Clenching the bed sheets in my fists with his head between my knees, I pray I'm not suffocating him. Then, he sucks my clit hard while thrusting two more fingers that expertly pump into me, and I come undone with a scream. My whole body goes numb, even my face tingles from the release.

After I've come down from my high, Delano crawls up to my face, bracing himself on his elbows. He wipes stray hairs from my eyes and then kisses me fiercely, bringing feeling back into my face. I feel completely blissed out, but I want to keep exploring him at the same time.

"How was that?" he asks, flashing me a knowing smirk.

I giggle and sigh. "I have no words. That was incredible. "

"Hmm," he hums in delight. "I'd happily bury my face between your legs all day, every day," he says. "Unfortunately, we should get going."

"What about you?" I ask.

"I'd happily let you do whatever you want to me, but we can't miss our flight," he says with a groan.

I nod. "I'm going to shower real quick. Do you need to use the bathroom?" I ask, nervous about how to handle whatever this is after the intimacy we just shared.

"I'll follow you in," he says as he stands and offers me his hand. I get up and lead us into my bathroom. It's tiny compared to what he's probably used to, but I try to push the thought out of my mind.

While I wait for the water to warm up, we stand at the counter, looking into the mirror at each other.

"Look at us," he says, and I take a moment to really take our reflection in. We really do look good together: such opposites, his strong lines and dark features contrasting against my fair skin and lighter hair, yet somehow, we complement each other.

He wraps his arms around me from behind, and I lean back into his chest. He kisses the side of my head, keeping his eyes locked with mine in comfortable silence.

My heart beats wildly in my chest; I'm so scared this can't last. There are so many reasons why this can only end in heartbreak for me, with him living in England and me inevitably returning to New York. I can't let my heart lead me astray from my career.

Somehow, despite this thing between us feeling like so much more, I need to make sure Delano understands this can only be a short-term fling. Maybe someday, after I retire in a few years, we could make this work, but I can't expect a man like Delano to wait around.

I should have had that conversation with him before we got intimate. The way he's looking at me right now says he's falling just as hard as I am, and I need to slow this down before we both get hurt.

The Land of Snow

Delano

The look she's giving me mirrors my own feelings, and it scares me. There's a reason I don't date— most women cannot be trusted to not only want me for my money.

Yet, here I am, falling hard for her.

I don't want her out of my sight. I feel feral, possessive.. When Mark touched her, my blood boiled, and it took everything in me not to choke him out until he begged Clara for her forgiveness. This need to protect her is unlike anything I've felt before, greater than my need to breathe.

For some reason, I trust her. Maybe it's because she has her own career that she's obviously passionate about. She doesn't need me, which should be comforting, but damn, do I want her to need me. I've always been turned off from love, and the idea of dedicating myself to one person usually makes my stomach turn. Love seems to always lead to pain, and I couldn't handle any more pain in my life. No one has ever been worth the risk.

Until Clara. *My* Clara.

I can't get the image of her laid out before me out of my mind. Her body was so responsive to me, and I'm eager to see how else I can make her squirm.

When we arrived, she was shocked to see my personal plane. Her eyes were saucer-wide as we boarded and I showed her around the cabin, her excitement only spurring on my own.

She fell asleep next to me shortly after departure, her head against my shoulder, my hand on her toned thigh. Her soft breathing caresses my neck, helping to take my mind off the anxiety I feel every time I fly. I had an expected fear of plane crashes growing up, but therapy and being forced to jet set all over the world to open new hotels helped.

Despite having conquered my fear, I still struggle during landings. My palms get sweaty and my heart beats slightly too fast. The plane starts its descent, and I take another swig of whiskey to help ease the anxiety. I don't want Clara to see me like this.

I kiss her forehead, and her eyes flutter open.

"Are we almost there?" she asks me, her voice groggy, the sweetest sound. She lifts her head off my shoulder, and I instantly miss her warmth. I watch as she gracefully bends her back, arching it while reaching her arms up to stretch.

I raise up the window cover so she can see outside. The plane has just started its descent below the clouds, and you can see the city below. "See for yourself," I say, and she leans over my lap to look out.

"Wow, it's already dusted in snow," she says with bright eyes.

"Winter comes early here," I respond.

"I love it. It'll get me into the Nutcracker spirit!" she giggles. I love how excitable she gets at the little things. I need that infectious joy in my life.

The plane experiences some turbulence while descending, and my knuckles go white with how hard I'm gripping the arm rests. Clara must notice, because she gently puts her hand over mine and squeezes. With her other hand, she caresses the side of my face, bringing my focus to her. She moves her hand around to the back of my neck, pulling my lips to hers as she kisses me softly.

As soon as our lips meet, I get lost in her, forgetting all about landing. I grab her around her waist and lift her onto my lap so she's straddling me, brushing her hair out of her face and whispering "thank you" before crashing my lips to hers again. The little moans she makes when I suck on her bottom lip and tangle my tongue with hers are my undoing. I'm painfully hard as she starts to grind against my lap, seeking out her own friction.

A loud ding rings through the cabin, and the lights grow brighter as the captain announces our arrival in London. We both freeze, chests heaving, resting our foreheads against each other, and she lets out a little giggle as she slides back over into her seat.

I groan inwardly, wishing we could've continued. I'm painfully aware that our time will be limited as soon as she starts rehearsing, not to mention all the work I've been ignoring.

I gather our luggage and lead us down to the tarmac, where my car awaits us. Clara stops in front of my emerald green F-Type Jaguar, and her jaw drops. I bundle our bags into the trunk and then open the passenger door for her. She hesitates, as if afraid to touch it, so I put my hand on the small of her back and usher her in.

"The car won't bite," I say with a wink.

"I've just never been in a car this fancy before," she says shyly.

"It's just a car," I tease with a shrug. I round the front to the driver's seat, turning the engine on, hearing that familiar purr. I love this car; as much as I don't usually like to be flashy with my money, I'm glad she's impressed. I get the feeling that Clara has been so focused on her career, she hasn't let herself live. I was like that at first, but I've learned to indulge more in recent years, and now, all I want to do is spoil her with everything I have. From what I can tell, she deserves it. She works her ass off every day.

As we drive, snow starts to fall, and Clara seems lost in her own thoughts, staring out her window with a smile. I love that we don't feel the need to fill the void of silence with needless talking, that we can just sit and be. It's so refreshing. Still, I do need to be touching her, which is why I have my hand on her thigh, drawing tiny figure eights with my thumb.

When we arrive at my hotel, the valet greets us at the curb.

"Good evening, Mr. Hoffman and Ms. Stahl. We will take your things to your individual suites." Clara looks up at him with a furrowed brow and then back at me, slightly thrown off by him knowing her name. I, of course, called ahead and made sure they had everything ready for her, so I just give her a shrug and a wink.

"Thank you, Ralph," I say, giving him a generous tip, as always.

"You're welcome, sir. We're glad you're home."

I usher Clara inside the lobby and watch as she takes in the modern grandeur. We design our hotels to be sleek but luxurious, welcoming but grand.

"I can't believe this is where you live,' she says. "I feel very under dressed in my leggings and sweater."

"You're the most beautiful thing here," I say, and it's true, even though she might not agree as she gives me an exaggerated eye roll.

I lead us to my private elevator for the penthouse apartments. "Do you need me to remind you just how beautiful you are?" I ask, and she just stares back at me from the opposite side of the elevator, biting her lower lip. "Because I won't have you thinking otherwise. I also won't have you talking negatively about yourself. That kind of behavior will have consequences," I say sternly.

"Consequences?" she asks in the quietest voice.

I stalk towards her, bracing my hands on either side of her hips against the railing. I lean in and lick up her neck to her earlobe, nipping gently before whispering in her ear. "I will bend you over my knee and spank your perfect ass red if you ever speak badly about yourself again," I say gruffly right before the elevator door dings. I walk out without a glance back, leaving her panting after me.

"My penthouse is on the left, and yours is on the right. I hope we can spend time together in one of them, but I also know the importance of having your own space, since you'll be in London until Christmas. Do you want me to give you a tour and order us food, or do you need to rest?" I ask, hoping she doesn't hide from me now that we're here. I almost didn't even give her her own space, selfishly wanting all of her spare time to myself.

"Food would be wonderful, but I really don't need an entire penthouse suite. I can take a regular hotel room just like anyone else would get," she argues.

"I disagree, Clara. You deserve the world, and I intend to give it to you, even if just for tonight," I say, and I watch as her pupils dilate as I bring her hand to my mouth and kiss her knuckles. "Go freshen up. I'll leave the door open for you. No one else can access this floor, so you don't need to worry about closing or locking doors."

She nods, and I watch her leave before entering my suite. Am I manipulating my ability to see her while she's in London by having her across the hall from me? Yes, I am. I know she'll be busy every day rehearsing, and I didn't want to leave seeing her again up to chance. I intend to make this evening memorable enough for her to want to keep seeing me, even if it's just in the evenings after work. I can't go on without knowing she's in my life and yet, there's so much doubt that this could ever be more than a fling. I'm struggling to see how we could make a real go of this when both of us have such demanding careers an ocean apart.

The Enchanted Palace

CLARA

Someone pinch me. This hotel is unreal. I'm not sure what I was expecting, but this is the most luxurious hotel I've ever been in. I had to stop myself from squealing as I explored the penthouse.

The first thought that went through my head was that I could get used to this. I've always loved hotels, joking that I could happily live in one, and here's Delano, doing exactly that and making me feel things I shouldn't. I really need to stop dreaming of an impossible life together.

This is why I don't date. It's just not possible right now, not with my grueling schedule. I'm so close to finally getting promoted to a principal dancer–I shouldn't be entertaining any distractions, and Delano is a *major* distraction.

A distraction I'm finding harder and harder to resist.

Why did I have to meet him now, of all times? Why couldn't we have met five years from now, when I'm closer to retirement? Then, I could jet all over the world with him. Instead, if we were to try to make this work, we would never see each other. I'd be busy rehearsing and performing in New York, and he'd be here in London or visiting his other hotels all over Europe. What's the point in even trying?

I just need to enjoy the time we have and guard my stupid heart from falling for him.

After freshening up in the luxurious, massive bathroom–complete with a gold, freestanding soaker tub that I will definitely be using every night after rehearsals–I change into a long sleeve, black sweater dress, the soft material hugging my body. It's sexy yet comfortable, and it feels right for a relaxing evening with Delano. I pull my thick hair into a high ponytail and forego makeup, just wearing tinted chapstick to let my skin breathe.

The bedroom is perfect, with dark teal walls, gold crown molding, and dark burgundy velvet drapes framing the floor-to-ceiling windows that look out onto the bustling city below. It's glorious, something I would design myself if budget were no object. Professional ballet dancers make just enough to survive in the big city. Dancing has never been about money or fame for me–the feeling of being on stage and telling a story through my body is what I live for. Still, having this kind of money must be nice.

I leave my suite and head across the hall. As Delano said, the door is open, and I'm assaulted with so many delicious smells when I walk in that I start salivating. I follow them to his kitchen, where I find him standing at the dining table, opening a bottle of wine.

"Hello, beautiful," he greets me, setting the wine down and coming over to kiss me on the cheek. He slides his arm around my waist, and as he pulls back, his hand grazes my ass. My cheeks flush and breath catches, just from the slightest touch.

"It smells amazing in here. What did you order?" I ask, seeing seven platters covered by silver lids.

"Just a few of my favorites from the restaurant downstairs, plus some desserts to share," he says with a coy smile while pulling out one of the chairs for me. He walks around the table to sit directly across from me and pours us both a nice, full glass of red wine. We dig in, and I can't help but moan at how good it all is. Pasta may be my first love.

The stereotype that ballerinas starve themselves is, unfortunately, partially true. I've known plenty of dancers who deny themselves the pleasures of real meals in exchange for scraps out of fear. My own eating habits have thankfully not been affected by those dangerous thoughts. I fucking *love* food, and I will not be shamed otherwise.

As we eat, Delano tells me about all the sights he wants to take me to while I'm here. I try to tame the excitement at us spending so much time together over the next month. I'm scared; I can't get too attached to him.

"Clara?" Delano says, and I realize it's been a minute since he finished talking.

"Hmm?" I say, not quite sure what he said, too busy thinking about how this thing between us is destined for disaster.

"Where did you go just then? You're lost in that brilliant mind of yours," he says with a furrowed brow. "Is there somewhere in London you want to see that I haven't mentioned?"

"Oh no, everything you've mentioned sounds wonderful. I'm just... well, I'm a little worried about being here with you and spending so much time together when I'll be leaving," I admit. I stare down at my plate and twirl pasta around on my fork, trying not to look him in the eye and see his disappointment.

"Clara. Look at me," he demands with his deep, velvety voice. I'm not usually someone who likes being told what to do, but when he speaks, I am like putty in his hands. His gaze is piercing as he leans in closer. "I know our time is limited, but that's why I want to make the most of it. You captivate me, and I can't have you in my city and not see you."

I should say no. I should set boundaries and protect myself; I already know he's going to break my heart. I should walk away, and yet, when I stare into his eyes, I can't move. I'm sucked into this vortex where all I see—all I want—is him.

"Okay. I'll let you show me this city of yours, but this thing between us has to stay casual. No pressure. No strings attached," I say, throwing up my walls where they belong.

Kingdom of Sweets

DELANO

"Well, I think we're already past casual," I drawl, trying to hide the growing disappointment in my gut. "But I agree with the rest. We're just enjoying each other and London," I say with a smirk that makes her blush. "Now that that's settled, let's have dessert." I get up and open the fridge, bringing out a silver tray full of specialty desserts from all over Europe.

"Oh my God. Where did you get all of that?" she asks, practically squealing. I set the tray down in front of her, opting to sit next to her now as I pick up a gingerbread cookie and bring it to her lips.

"Take a bite of this," I say, holding it up so she can take a bite. She does so without hesitation, and I have to admit, I love how submissive she is with me. I'm not a controlling person, but in intimate moments, I like to be in charge. Her tongue darts out to lick her lips, and my cock hardens as I wonder what it would be like to have them wrapped around me. My dirty thoughts turn into an inferno by the loud moan she makes when she takes a bite of chocolate mousse cake.

I can't take not touching her any longer, and I push my chair back so I can pull her into my lap. She squeals, giving me an incredulous look, to which I just shrug my shoulders and gesture for her to keep enjoying her desserts. I save my personal favorite for last: dark chocolate-dipped strawberries. I tease her, bringing a berry to her lips to taste and then pulling it away. She giggles, and every time she does, I lightly slap her perky ass, making her breath catch.

"Stop teasing and let me take a bite," she whines.

"I think not," I say as I trace her lips with the strawberry and then bring it to my mouth. She pouts, her plump bottom lip jutting out, and I can't help but chuckle. "Tell me how badly you want it. Beg for it, and I'll give it to you," I urge. With the fuck me eyes she's giving me, we both know we're not just talking about the strawberries anymore.

She grips the bottom of her black dress, slowly lifting it up and over her head before tossing it on the floor. Swallowing becomes difficult as I drag my eyes down her body.

"So beautiful," I whisper as I take her in. She stands before me in only a matching black lace bralette and thong, her body a work of art that I'm more than willing to worship.

I reward her with a bite of a strawberry, my restraint snapping when the juice drips down her chin, and I quickly lick it up.

I grab her by her thighs and hoist her up around my hips. She's so light in my arms, but she grips my waist with legs made of pure muscle, and I groan. We devour each other's mouths with deep, messy, tongue-tangled kisses; I love that I can taste the chocolate and wine. I walk her down the hall to my bedroom, groaning into her mouth as I went.

I lower us onto my bed, carefully cradling her between my forearms. Both our chests heave as we stare into each other's eyes. There's something so magnetic about our connection. Clara gives me the sweetest smile I've ever seen, and I wish I could take a picture to capture it forever. Her smile reminds me of sunshine peering through the clouds after it rains. I know our moments are limited, and I just want to savor this—*her*.

"Tell me what you want," I whisper, though with the way she grinds her hips into mine, trying to find friction, I already know.

She surprises me by reaching down and palming my cock through my pants. It dawns on me that she's nearly naked, and I'm still fully clothed in my suit.

"I want all of you, but I'm a little worried you won't fit," she says softly, biting on her lower lip.

I smirk, standing to undo my tie and toss it aside. "You have nothing to worry about. I know you can take it," I say as I unbutton my shirt. Clara props herself up on her elbows and watches me undress with a hungry glint in her eyes. She likes what she sees, if that cute little quirk of her mouth and lick of her lips are any indication. While I don't build vanity muscles, I run and lift weights to help keep my mind quiet when things feel too chaotic. I played futbol all through school, and I still have my six pack abs.

Once I'm fully undressed, I kneel down in front of the bed. Grabbing her hips, I pull her ass to the edge, which earns me another sexy giggle.

"Lift your hips, baby," I say, and I pull off her thong, already damp with her arousal. I take in her beautiful bare pink pussy, and my eyes roll back at the perfect sight. My hands roam up to her tits, the shape of them made just to fit in my hands. I tweak her nipples through the lace of her bra, making her buck into my mouth. I take my time torturing her clit, alternating between licking, sucking and nibbling. I absolutely love the smell and taste of her; she's an addiction so sweet, I don't know how I could ever have another after.

It doesn't take long before she's squeezing my head between her thighs, screaming my name as she comes all over my face. I make my way up her body, peppering kisses along the way. I want to devour every inch of her. Her skin tastes sweet, like a damn sugar cookie. *One only I get to taste.* Her arm is tossed over her head, her face hiding in the crook of her elbow. I can't have that.

"Eyes on me, baby," I tell her as I take her hands in mine, intertwining our fingers and bringing them to either side of her head. She gives me those big, beautiful, brown doe eyes and smiles shyly. I can feel her heartbeat pounding against my chest, and I love that I can make her come undone so quickly. "You taste better than any dessert I've ever had," I tell her as her cheeks go red. "Are you still up for more, or do you want to rest?"

"More, definitely more," she says eagerly as she lifts her head to kiss me. She explores my mouth with hers, making me moan deeper into the kiss. I nudge her legs apart with my knees, making room for me to line myself up with her center. My cock is weeping for her and with how wet she is for me, I know I could easily slip in despite her worry I won't fit.

I swipe the head of my cock up and down between her lips, using her slick to ready myself for her. She's making the most heavenly little moans, and as soon as she angles her hips up, greedy for me, I know she's ready. Slowly, I slide just my tip into her as I rub her clit with my thumb. She bucks up, urging me to keep going.

Taking my time, I push in to the hilt, rising up on my hands to watch her. She's so tight, the fit so perfect, I'm fighting every urge to ravage her before she gets used to my size.

"Oh. My. God..." she gasps. "You feel so good." She moans while arching her back, grabbing my ass cheeks with both hands to grind harder, deeper against me.

"Fuck," I curse, trying to tether my restraint. She's a damn dream. I pull out and push back in slowly before completely getting lost in her heat. We make a mess of the sheets, moving between different positions effortlessly. She's so damn flexible, moving easily as I lift her legs to rest them on my chest, and when I lean forward, they bend with ease, her knees practically straddling her head while I pound into her.

When I move her on top, the sweet side of Clara is gone as she rides me hard. Her long, golden-brown hair flows wildly around her shoulders, reminding me of the paintings I've seen of Greek goddesses. Her gorgeous breasts are on full display as she uses me to chase her pleasure, and I can't imagine a more beautiful sight.

We lock eyes as she comes again, chanting my name. Feeling her shatter on top of me makes me pump into her fast and hard, and then I'm following her over the edge. I yell out as I come deep inside her, enjoying the way she shudders as my cock twitches with my release. She collapses onto me, resting her head on my chest. I wrap my arms around her tiny waist, not wanting this moment to end. *Not wanting anything about us to ever end*, I finally admit to myself.

How can I ever let her walk away at the end of December? It's absolutely unfathomable in this moment. This will never be enough. There's no getting her out of my system. I'm addicted, and I need to figure out how to get her to stay.

An Arabian Dance

CLARA

Over the next few weeks, Delano and I fall into a comfortable rhythm. We wake up early, usually with him kissing my neck and slowly fucking me awake before we have coffee together.

He makes the most amazing coffee, a method he learned during his time in the Middle East. After we enjoy our coffee, I get ready for days full of ballet class and rehearsals, and he heads to his company's headquarters. I'm usually the first one to return, generally napping before he gets home.

Home. I can't believe that's what it feels like, but I can't deny it. Ever since my first night here, I've stayed with him in his penthouse, the one across the way basically becoming where I store my things.

I know I should be guarding my heart. We shouldn't be playing house, but I can't pull away, despite how my brain screams at me to put up more walls. My heart wins the argument everytime. I know I've already fallen in love with him, and I convince myself that the pain to come will be worth it—nothing has ever felt so good.

I'm in love with London, too. Anytime we get time off together, he plays my personal tour guide. He takes me to all the must-see spots, as well as his personal favorites. From strolling through cobblestone streets to visiting iconic landmarks, I can't help but marvel at the rich tapestry of the city.

My favorite thing, though, is how decked out the city is for Christmas. I never thought anything could beat New York City, with its decorations and Bryant Park Christmas market, but I was wrong. London is on a whole other level of holiday cheer, and I am here for it.

During our adventures, I discovered a different side of Delano. He's so much more than a broody billionaire hotel tycoon, even though I knew that the moment I met him. He opened up about his own personal struggles and triumphs, allowing me a glimpse into the complex layers defining him. Our conversations have become a cherished refuge from the whirlwind of my ballet rehearsals, and I think, other than the mind blowing sex, they're what I'll miss the most—walking aimlessly through the city streets, lost in conversation or comfortable silence with him.

My whole life has been ballet, but seeing what life could be like with Delano makes me wonder if it's what I really want, if it could be possible to dream outside of the dance world.

Tonight, as we lay in Delano's bed, our bodies intertwined in each other's embrace, the world outside fades away. We easily lose ourselves in each other's touch, our connection deepening with every kiss. In these moments, I allow myself to dream, to envision a future where this is my forever. *Where he is my forever.*

I can picture a life filled with love, support, and shared dreams. Images of us strolling through London's parks, attending art exhibitions, and exploring the hidden corners of the world together dance in my mind as I fall asleep in his arms. The whisper of possibility tugs at my heart, and a tear escapes down my cheek as I yearn for a future I know can't be mine.

***

I wake up happy that it's the weekend, and I happen to not have any classes or rehearsals today. With opening night only a couple weeks away, I want to soak up all the free time I have with Delano. Once the shows start, I'll practically be living at the theater, sometimes performing two times a day.

I absolutely love working with London Ballet. The director, Madame Ginger, is so kind, with so much artistry. I'm learning so much from her, and I can't help but compare how different it is from working with Mark. The other dancers have been so welcoming to me and my partner Trevor. I haven't come across anyone like Emily, and it's quite refreshing.

"Good morning," Delano says as he walks in with coffee for each of us. It's my favorite time of day with him, just lounging in bed together without a care in the world.

"Good morning, handsome," I respond, loving the smile that lights up his face. I honestly don't think he realizes just how good looking he is. He's pretty humble, which surprises me.

He hands me my coffee and kisses the top of my head as he gets back into bed.

"I have a surprise for you," he says with a coy smile.

"Really? I love surprises," I say. He's constantly spoiling me, and I'd be lying if I said I didn't love it. I've never had a man put me first in so many ways. I only hope he knows how much I appreciate him.

"Good. You'll need to pack a bag and be ready to leave in an hour," he says nonchalantly.

"Are you going to tell me where we're going?" I ask, staring at him with wide eyes. "I need to know how to pack."

"It'll be cold, but warmer than here, and no snow," he says. "It'll just be two nights, since you have to be back Tuesday for rehearsals. That's all I'm telling you until we get there."

I let out an audible sigh, except I'm grinning ear to ear–I'm so excited to get away with him. I fly out of bed and race across the hall to start packing, my body buzzing with excitement as I think of all the places it could be.

Two hours later, we land in the enchanting city of Barcelona. Once we arrived, Delano explained that he opened up a hotel here last year and needed to check in. At first, I was disappointed that it was a work trip, but he promised me that the only work was seeing how comfortable the bed in the penthouse suite was.

A private car drives us from the airport to the hotel, and I can't help but stare out the window, marveling at the eclectic mix of medieval and modern buildings we pass.

"I've never seen anything like it," I say, practically squealing with excitement. I've always dreamed of traveling through Europe. "How many times have you been to Spain?" I ask, curious to know more about his work. He's shared bits here and there, and from what I can tell, he mostly has constant meetings and people reporting to him at all hours of the day.

"Only a few times, most of which were when I was scouting out locations," he says. "But there's a reason I wanted to bring you here, of all the hotels I could've taken you to," he says with that smirk that gives me butterflies every time.

"Oh? Why's that?" I ask, trying to play it cool.

"One word: *chocolate*," he says, in such a seductive way that my thighs clench and I lick my lips. He scoots closer, until our legs are touching and he can lean to whisper in my ear. "My favorite is the melted chocolate, and I can't wait to lick it off of you." He kisses my neck before sliding back over, leaving me breathless and my whole body tingling from his words.

When we arrive at the hotel, I nearly gasp at the beautiful medieval palace before me. We enter the elegant lobby with parquet flooring and a gloriously painted stuccoed ceiling. Delano leads me to our suite, where windows reveal breathtaking panoramas of the city. The room itself is luxurious, but with more modern furniture and art than the London hotel. Before we even have a chance to freshen up, Delano playfully tosses me onto the bed.

"First things first: we need to test this bed out right away," he says, and I can't help the giggles that escape my lips. He stands over me, slowly undoing his tie and then unbuttoning his crisp dress shirt that probably costs more than my entire wardrobe. We haven't talked about the fact that he's one of the world's youngest billionaires, which I learned from a late night session with Google. It's a bit intimidating, and I try to pretend like it's not a big deal, but sometimes, I wonder what he's doing with me when he could have anyone he wants.

I'm distracted from my thoughts when he sheds his shirt and reveals his toned chest and abs. I've seen him naked plenty of times now, but his sculpted body never fails to leave me in awe.

"See something you like, Sugarplum?" I smile wide at the nickname, loving the devilish grin he's giving me.

The Land of Chocolate

DELANO

She stares up at me like I'm a tasty morsel she wants to lick, and I can't help but chuckle. She brings out a playful side of me that I've kept buried since I was a young boy. Everything about her makes me feel free, and I'd do anything to make her laugh. She lights up the entire room when she smiles, and I'll never get enough of it.

As she nods in response to my question, she sits up and scoots to the edge of the bed, reaching for my belt. I watch with bated breath as she undoes it slowly before unbuttoning and unzipping my pants. I can't help but rub my thumb over her bottom lip, pulling it down. She playfully nips at my thumb, and my cock becomes unbearably hard at the sight.

"Get on your knees for me, baby," I command. She turns away from me, getting down on her hands and knees, glancing back at me while wiggling her backside. Her arse is a work of art; her glutes defined, and her cheeks so perky, I want to bite them. So I do, making her gasp and then moan deeply.

"God damn, Clara. It's taking all my restraint to not ravish you completely, but I have other plans," I groan as I take her in. "Stay right where you are. I'll be right back."

I quickly walk to the kitchen and grab the tray of Spanish chocolates I had sent to our room before our arrival. On it is a pot of *chocolate caliente,* which is like hot chocolate but much thicker and much more delicious. I dip my finger in to test that it's not too hot before heading back to the bedroom.

I find Clara in the same position, but she's resting her head on top of her hands, making her bottom stick up in the air with her sex on full display. I groan at the sight.

"You are a goddess."

She looks back at me, biting her lip and eyeing the tray. "What's all that?" she asks curiously.

"It's why I wanted to bring you to Spain," I say, setting the tray down next to her on the bed. "The best chocolate in the world is from here, and knowing what a sweet tooth you have, I couldn't deny you the chance to try it," I explain, smiling as I watch her face light up in anticipation.

"So you were actually serious in the car?" she asks.

"Completely."

I grab a piece of dark chocolate and take a bite, holding it between my front teeth. I lean over on the bed, propping myself up on my elbow in front of Clara as I bring my mouth close to hers. She takes a nibble, moaning at the intense flavor before sealing her lips to mine, stealing the rest of the piece from my mouth while our tongues dance around the melting chocolate.

"Like it?" I ask as I use my thumb to wipe some of the chocolate from her lips. I bring it to my mouth and lick it off.

"Love it," she answers, her beautiful eyes twinkling up at me. For a moment, I wonder if she means me or the chocolate, but I shake those thoughts out of my head. This can't be love. It's too soon, and she's made it clear that she's going back to New York no matter what. This is just for fun, I remind myself, even though it feels like so much more.

"You're such a good girl, waiting so patiently on your hands and knees for me," I tell her as I get up and make my way back behind her, careful to not let the tray tip. "And good girls get more chocolate," I say with a smirk.

I reach for the pot of melted chocolate and ever so slowly pour it onto her back, from the base of her neck down her spine. Then, starting at the top of her arse, I lick my way up her back, taking my time. Goosebumps break out across her skin, and she rubs her thighs together, looking for friction. When I get to the back of her neck, I take the last lick, but instead of swallowing it down, I grab her chin and kiss her so she can have a taste. We both moan, and I can't wait any longer to have her.

Sitting back, I line myself up with her entrance, feeling how wet and ready she is for me before pushing into the hilt. Wrapping her hair around my hand to keep her from moving forward from the force of my thrusts, I lean over her, kissing her shoulders and neck. I reach around to rub her clit with my other hand, all the chocolate foreplay having us both coming undone much more quickly.

I can feel her squeezing me tightly as she starts to quiver beneath me, her orgasm coming hard and fast. She arches her back, lifting up to her knees as she wraps her arms around my neck to kiss me through it.

I wrap my hands around her heaving breasts, holding onto them as my own release barrels into her. I nearly black out from the force of it, and once again, I'm blown away by how incredible it is to be with her. We collapse onto the bed, tangled up together, coming down from the high. We lay there for a while, chests heaving. I've never been one for post-coital kissing or touching, let alone cuddling, but with Clara, I crave it. I reach over her stomach, grabbing her hand in mine as I intertwine our fingers.

It's in these moments that those three little words sit on the tip of my tongue, but I stop myself. We promised to not get feelings involved, and I don't want to scare her off by telling her otherwise.

"So, what's next?" she asks cheerfully.

"A shower."

She rolls her eyes at me and playfully slaps my chest. "You know what I mean. When do we get to explore?"

"After we shower," I say with a wink as I peel myself out of bed.

***

For the next two days, I take Clara on a tour through Barcelona. We indulge in the best food and drinks that the city has to offer, savoring the decadence and history around us. As we stroll hand in hand through the narrow streets of the Gothic Quarter, our laughter and intimate conversations fill the air.

Each evening, we dine at charming restaurants, savoring the flavors of Spain. In the quiet moments, as we watch the sunset over the Mediterranean Sea each night from our hotel room, our connection seems to grow even deeper. It's all made me realize how much richer a life with her could be. In such a short amount of time, she's become my best friend, my lover, my everything. I'm beginning to hate the fact that we can't be more, but I try to stay in the present with her, to soak it up as much as possible.

Yet, I can't help the sinking feeling that all this time together will amount to nothing, and I'll be back to being the lonely bastard I've been for the last two decades.

Pas de Deux with the Prince

Clara

After bidding farewell to Barcelona and returning to London, I found myself more confused than ever. Being there with him and seeing him so carefree brought us so much closer, which only complicates things. If only I was staying in London, or Delano's work took him to New York more often—I'd jump at the chance to further our relationship. Knowing we have an expiration date makes this insane connection so much harder to navigate. It doesn't feel like it should end, but we both know it will.

Despite this, we can't seem to stop ourselves from acting like a real couple. We're practically living together, and no matter how much I tell myself to pull away, I just can't. It's like we're two magnets that refuse to be pulled apart. Every time I convince myself I need to talk to him about it, that I'm going to start staying at the penthouse across the hall, I just can't bring myself to do it.

I'm in love with him, and I don't know how to stop my foolish heart from falling further.

***

The weeks pass and December arrives, bringing with it the night of the Nutcracker gala. Delano attends as my date, and I feel giddy with him at my side. A week ago, Delano brought me to a designer he knows who fitted me for a custom gown. It's a lovely red, spaghetti strap gown covered in beading that hugs my hourglass figure. We barely made it on time because Delano couldn't keep his hands off me.

We enter the ballroom of Delano's hotel, and I hold onto his arm tightly. I had no idea that his company sponsors the event each year. It's expertly decorated like a winter wonderland, with crystal snowflakes dangling from the ceiling and massive, fake snow-covered pine trees spread throughout. He expertly leads me through the crowds to our table as I suppress my nerves. It's the first time I'm attending an event like this as a guest artist, and I'm trying my hardest not to fidget.

"Okay, I just got really nervous," I whisper in his ear. I feel like all eyes are on us. We continue walking, only stopping so he can shake a few people's hands along the way.

"Well, you *are* the most stunningly beautiful creature in this room, so I'm not surprised that all eyes are on you," he whispers back as we finally reach our table. I'm not so sure that they aren't all staring at him, in his tuxedo that fits him like a glove. "They can all look at you, but don't forget that you're mine," he says, making my heart flutter. I wish it was true that he could keep me forever, but I know he means just for now.

I'm thrilled to see his grandparents already seated, their faces filled with pride and admiration. My dance partner, Trevor, and his husband Cameron are already seated as well. Everyone stands to greet us, and we talk amongst ourselves as dinner is served. It's nice to be a guest dancer, to enjoy the event and not have to do the entertaining for once.

After dinner, Delano's grandfather pulls him away to talk with some business associates, and since Trevor and Cameron are on the dance floor, I'm left sitting with Delano's grandmother.

"My grandson is smitten with you, I see," she says with a curious smile. "Not that I'm surprised. You're such a lovely girl."

"Thank you. I find him quite lovely as well," I admit, feeling my cheeks flush.

"Such a shame you're leaving after the Nutcracker season. I'm worried our Delano will be quite heartbroken," she says, pinning me with her eyes, awaiting a response. I wish I could ease her fears, but she's spot on.

"Well, if it's any consolation, I'll probably be more heartbroken than he is," I say quietly, worried he will come back any minute and hear this conversation. We haven't talked about our feelings—more like avoiding them—but when we're in each other's arms every night, I know we both feel it.

She cocks her head to the side, observing me, and I have to look away so that I don't break down and cry. She reaches over and grabs my hand, squeezing it gently. "My grandson's an idiot if he lets you go," she says with a wink. All I can do is sadly smile back, because I'm not sure she's correct. Maybe *I'm* the idiot for leaving.

Final Waltz

DELANO

I stare at Clara from across the room and can't deny how deeply I feel for her. I should be listening to the conversation my grandfather is having, but I can't take my eyes off her. Every day, I wake up and tell myself that I'll pull away, but instead, I find myself consumed by her, body and soul.

I'm at the point where I'm ready to confess my feelings and beg for her to stay. I don't care about the constraints of time and distance anymore–the thought of not having her in my life far outweighs any prior hesitations. Still, there's a small inkling of fear that she isn't willing to take the risk holding me back.

I know her career is important to her, and I wouldn't want to get in the way of that, but I also know that she seems to be thriving with the London Ballet. I can't help but hope she wants to stay and join their company instead. In fact, I've taken it upon myself to meet with the director about the possibility, and she's hoping the same thing. She plans to make Clara the offer after the first night's performance, which is why tonight, I plan to tell

Clara I'm in love with her so she knows just how badly I want her to stay.

I excuse myself from the conversation to make my way over to Clara when an unwelcome and unexpected visitor in the form of a rodent named Mark walks up to her. My grandmother still sits with her, so hopefully, he keeps his hands to himself. I see Clara tense, and all my muscles do the same. I increase my pace to get to her sooner, but it seems like everyone tries to stop me to say hello. I play nice, shaking hands and giving nods. I try to keep walking towards them, and yet I'm lost in a sea of ball gowns. I lose sight of our table, and my blood boils as I clench my jaw in frustration.

By the time I get to her, Mark is gone, and surprisingly, Clara has a smile beaming across her face. Confusion and conflicting emotions wash over me.

I lean down and kiss her temple before taking my seat next to her. "I saw Mark and tried to get to you as fast as possible. Did he say or do anything inappropriate?" I ask, my fury at the sight of him still coursing through my veins. My grandmother gives me a strange, worried look, and my heart plummets into my stomach.

"Actually, quite the opposite," Clara says happily. "Mark apologized for his behavior in New York and said he was here to watch our opening night. He looks forward to making the announcement about my promotion immediately after." Her voice oozes with excitement, and I feel sick.

"What promotion?" I ask through gritted teeth. I know I should be happy for her, but all I feel is disappointment that I can't hide.

"To principal dancer," Clara says with hesitation, obviously picking up on my sour mood. "I've dreamed of this my whole life," she whispers.

Frustration clouds my mind as I take a deep breath, trying to figure out how to respond without scaring her off.

"Clara, these past months with you have been nothing short of extraordinary," I begin, my voice tinged with a vulnerability I honestly hate. "I believe we've found something special, something worth exploring further, and I had hoped there would be a way for us to be together, beyond our time in London. I didn't want to ruin the surprise, but the London Ballet is going to make you the same offer. You could stay here, and we could really make a go of this," I say, gently cupping Clara's cheek.

Clara's eyes widen with surprise, and I hold my breath, awaiting her answer.

"Delano, I feel it too," Clara confessed, her voice filled with tenderness. "These past few months have been incredible, and I can't deny the depth of my feelings for you. Still, I've only ever wanted to dance with American Ballet Company, and I don't know if I can give up that dream just yet."

"I get it, but dreams can shift and change. You'd still be fulfilling that dream, just here in London," I say, pulling away from her in frustration. "I honestly can't believe you would want to go back and dance for Mark after what he did to you. You're letting yourself be blinded by a childhood wish," I seethe in an angry whisper. I know it's harsh, but she needs to wake up. Mark is manipulating her.

A flicker of anger crosses Clara's face as she grasps my words. "Easy for you to say. You're not the one being asked to uproot your entire life," she says, her voice laced with bitterness. "How do you know London Ballet will be making me an offer anyway?"

"Last week, when I watched one of your rehearsals, I spoke with the director, and she told me then," I explain.

"Oh, I see, so they're doing you a favor. How do I know they really want me for me?" she asks, throwing her hands up and then crossing them over her chest. She stares at me, awaiting my answer, and I hate that I don't have a good one. It's our first true disagreement, a clash of dreams that threatens to tear at the fabric of our connection.

"Of course they want you for you. How could they not? You're incredible, and you deserve the promotion. ABC should have realized your potential sooner. Mark is just manipulating you because he doesn't want to lose you to them. It shouldn't have taken that to make him realize your worth," I say. "I'm begging you to think about it before making a decision," I whisper into her ear before standing. I think I need to give her some space so she can figure out what she wants.

"Where are you going?" she asks with tears in her eyes.

"I'm going to head home. Enjoy the evening. You deserve it," I say quietly. I walk over to the other side of the table. "Goodnight Grandmother," I say, kissing her cheek. She pulls me into a hug and whispers back, "Don't give up on her." I give her a tight smile and a nod before turning to walk away.

"Delano, wait," Clara calls out. I stop in my tracks and turn back around as she approaches me. "Please don't leave. I don't want to be here without you," she says as a tear runs down her cheek.

"That's exactly how I feel, beautiful," I whisper as I brush it away, my voice ridiculously full of emotion. I hate seeing her sad, but I don't know what else there is to say. I turn around, leaving her behind and hoping she doesn't hate me for it.

Dance of the Sugarplum Fairy

CLARA

I want to be angry at Delano, I really do, but back at the penthouse (mine, not his), not sleeping next to him is turning my anger into remorse. I lay down in the big, cold bed, rehashing Delano's words in my head. I can't deny that some of them hold weight.

I have dreamt of this promotion, to be recognized for my talent and dedication, with American Ballet Company for so long, I've been willing to overlook the wrongness that is Mark. I fully recognize how problematic that is, but it's the sad truth. When you fight for something your whole life, it's hard not to put blinders up along the way. I hate that Delano called me out on it, mostly because I'm embarrassed that it's true.

Then he had to go and tell me everything I've been wanting to hear from him these last few weeks. He wants to explore a future together, and I do too, but I'm scared at the same time. I don't want to be one of those girls who gives everything up for love, yet I can't help but wonder if I'm allowing fear to guide my decisions.

A part of me doesn't believe I can have it all, since that's so rarely the case in the ballet world. Most professional dancers wait to get married and have children until after they retire. Our careers are just so short, very rarely going beyond our late thirties. I always figured love would come later. If I walk away from him, will I regret it forever? Or will I regret switching ballet companies more?

In the midst of these swirling thoughts and emotions, I long for clarity. Opening night as the Sugarplum Fairy is less than a week away, and I think the best thing would be to wait and see how I feel afterwards. There's no way to know if the London Ballet will actually make me the offer. It could be wishful thinking on Delano's part.

Even if I do get an offer to join their company, how do I know Delano and I would work out? He's never been in a committed relationship before, and both our careers are so intense; I'm not sure we could give each other what we deserve. I'd be living so far away from my parents and Gabby, the three people who mean the most to me other than Delano, but the thought of living a life without him has me falling asleep with a tear-soaked pillow.

***

I sit in my private dressing room after my first performance as Sugarplum surrounded by fragrant bouquets of flowers.

Dancers always have one role that they dream of, and Sugarplum has always been mine. It felt like a dream the entire time.

The director of London Ballet just left my room after personally congratulating me and making me an offer to join them. She mentioned all the incredible roles she thinks I would be perfect for in their upcoming season, and she assured me that the offer had nothing to do with my relationship with Delano but purely my abilities. I let her know that I was honored and needed time to consider before giving her my answer.

Despite our quarrel at the gala, Delano and I moved past it, and these last few days have been pure bliss. When I woke up the next morning, he had left a bouquet of daisies at the door with an apology note begging me to come back to his penthouse that night. When we got home that evening, we both apologized, and he promised he'd not push my decision, that he'd support me in whatever I decided. Still, I could see the hurt in his eyes that I spent the rest of the night trying to kiss away.

There's a knock at my door, and I call out, "Who is it?"

"It's me," Delano replies in that deep voice that makes my insides feel like jello. I don't know how a person can turn me on by just the tone of their voice, but he can.

I stand up from the vanity and cinch my silk robe around my waist before opening the door. As soon as I do, I see Delano leaning against the door frame, one leg crossed over the other, a massive bouquet of dark red roses in front of his face. He lowers them slowly, revealing the most dashing smile.

"You were magnificent," he says as he walks forward, guiding me back into the dressing room and kicking the door closed behind him.

"Thank you," I say as I grab the flowers and take a deep inhale before setting them down. I'd rather be holding onto him. As soon as the flowers are set aside, he grabs me by the waist and lifts me in the air. I brace my arms on his shoulders as we look deeply into each other's eyes.

He lowers me slowly, bringing our faces so close, our noses are touching. "I'm so fucking proud of you. I've seen dozens of Sugarplums, but none lit up the stage like you did tonight," he whispers, his voice gravelly and thick with emotion.

He gently sets me down, moving a few loose strands of hair behind my ear before kissing me soft and sweetly. I'm not sure which side of Delano I love more: the rough, demanding one, or the sweet, gentlemanly one. I'm addicted to both, and it's in these moments that I can't fathom leaving.

"Do we have time for me to worship you?" he asks as he kisses down my neck and sucks on my collarbone.

"I think so," I say, barely recognizing my voice–I can hardly think when he kisses me like this.

"How do you want it, baby? You're in charge here," he says.

I still have so much adrenaline flowing through me from my performance that his kisses have turned me on quickly, and I can't wait anymore.

"Hard and fast," I whisper as I turn around and brace my hands on the wall. That's all he needed to hear, apparently, before he lifts my robe up to my waist and slams fully into me from behind. He holds onto my hip with one hand and pinches my nipple through my robe with the other. I reach down and rub my clit, my moans getting louder as I push back against his hips, meeting him thrust for thrust.

"Yes, yes, just like that," I say, my voice growing frantic as I feel the familiar wave of my orgasm rushing in. "I'm coming. Oh, God. Yes," I shout as he grabs my chin, turning my head and kissing me through it.

His own release follows shortly after as he whispers my name over and over like a prayer. He rests his head on my back, kissing my shoulder before pulling out. I hand him some tissues and we clean each other up.

He cradles my face in his hands, and we rest our foreheads together, letting our heart rates come down.

"Thank you," he murmurs sweetly.

A knock on my door pulls me out of the lavender haze. "Coming," I call out and reluctantly pull out of Delano's embrace. I open the door to find my parents standing on the other side, beaming at me with smiles full of pride. I had no idea they were coming, and when I see their faces, I realize just how much I've missed them.

"Clara!" my mother squeals as she pulls me into a hug. "You were magnificent, darling," she exclaims. "And Mr. Ratton just told us the exciting news that you've been promoted to principal, effective immediately. He already announced it on the company's social media. All your dreams have come true!"

My face pales, and I feel like I might vomit. I turn and look over my shoulder at Delano, only to find he looks the same, except more like he might commit murder with how clenched his jaw is.

"What? Oh... wow, that's..."

"Honey, your mother and I are so incredibly proud of you. You were exquisite. The perfect Sugarplum," my dad says as he kisses me on the cheek. They're so happy for me—I can't bring myself to tell them I might not accept the promotion. Except now that it's been announced without my official acceptance, I don't know if I can.

It's then that my parents realize I wasn't alone in my dressing room. "Oh, sorry. I didn't realize you had other visitors," my mom says coyly.

"Mom, Dad, this is Delano. He's a benefactor of both ABC and the London Ballet. We met back in New York, and he's been showing me all the sights the last couple of months. He's..." I hesitate, realizing we've been so caught up in each other that we've never really labeled *us*. "He's a dear friend," I say with a tight smile, suddenly feeling really insecure about *us*.

"It's lovely to meet you, Mr. and Mrs. Stahl. Your daughter is incredible and deserves all the accolades for her dancing. I'm shocked she wasn't promoted sooner," he says while shaking their hands. I know that was a dig at Mark, and I feel my stomach bottom out at the reality that Mark just took my choice to stay in London away. He's sealed my fate with his announcement, and by the pained look on Delano's face, he's realized the same thing. "I will let you all catch up. I should be going," he says, not looking me in the eye.

"It was nice to meet you. Thanks for looking out for our daughter in London," my dad says. Delano just nods and walks out, leaving so many words unspoken between us. I put on a happy face for my parents as we catch up, but inside, my heart feels like it's shattering.

Awakening from the Dream

DELANO

*F*riends.

I know she was probably thrown off having to explain our relationship to her parents, and maybe it's my fault for not asking her to be my girlfriend, but the word didn't seem good enough for what she is to me.

I want her to be my everything. My *partner*. My *wife*. My *forever*.

I leave the theater and exit onto the blustery streets, determined to walk home and let the freezing air cool the fire coursing through my veins. I can't believe the shit Mark pulled, announcing Clara's promotion before she gave him an answer. He knew what he was doing. He knew that if he put it out into the world, she would be forced to accept.

The idea of her leaving makes me feel physically ill. It was already going to be challenging, making a relationship work with her grueling dance schedule and my need to travel so often for work, but we could do it. Still, if she goes back to New York, I'm not sure our relationship is strong enough to survive. We simply haven't had enough time.

I have to convince her to turn down the promotion and stay. Screw Mark and his announcement. He can't dictate her life. She deserves so much better, and I need to help her realize that leaving is a mistake.

***

I'm not sure when Clara got home, but when I wake up to her body wrapped around mine, I let out a sigh of relief. I'm thankful she came back to my bed instead of retreating across the hall. As upset as I am about the possibility of her leaving, I need her to know that I'm not mad at her.

I trace lazy circles on her arm wrapped around my stomach. She stirs a little but still seems to be in a deep sleep. I check my watch on the side table to find it's ten in the morning, so hopefully, she's had enough sleep. She must be exhausted after her first performance last night. I still can't get over what a vision she was onstage. I hate that she's ever doubted herself as a dancer. She was made for it.

I always avoided dating dancers at all costs because I thought it would remind me of my parents. Yet with Clara, it only makes me feel more connected to my mother. I know she would have loved Clara, loved me being with a ballerina.

I turn onto my side so I'm facing her. She looks so peaceful as I use my finger to trace her delicate features, lightly brushing over her eyebrows, nose, and lastly, plump lips before kissing her, causing her eyelids to flutter open.

"Good morning, Sugarplum," I coo.

"Hi," she says with a lazy smile.

"Ready for coffee, or do you want to sleep longer?" I ask. I love getting up before her each morning and making us both coffee to bring back to bed. It's been one of our routines. Sometimes, we sip our coffee and talk or read. Other times, the coffee gets cold because we're too busy making love.

"Coffee," she says as she stretches her arms up in the most graceful way before sitting up against the headboard.

When I come back into the room with coffee in hand, Clara is looking at her phone like she's seen a ghost.

"What's wrong?"

"The news of my promotion has been leaked everywhere. My social media is full of congratulations and people wanting my statement or to book me for photoshoots and interviews for dance blogs and magazines," she explains before she tosses her phone aside. She buries her head in her hands, looking so defeated.

I quickly set down our coffee and crawl back into bed, wrapping my arms around her. She leans into me, and I can feel her tears against my chest. The shadows of doubt and uncertainty swirl around us as I just hold her.

As soon as Clara's calm and her tears have dried, I broach the topic gently, not wanting to upset her any further. I intertwine our fingers as I start the conversation we need to have but have both been dreading since last night.

"Clara, this may not be how I hoped things would go, but I understand the significance of this promotion, and I want you to be happy, to live your dream life," I begin, trying to sound as positive as possible. I expect to look at her and see relief, but she looks up at me with pain in her eyes.

"But that's just it, Delano: I think my dreams have changed," she says, lifting her head off my chest and cupping my jaw in her dainty hands. "My new dreams include you. I was going to accept London's offer. I want to be here with you," she says as a single tear streaks down her cheek.

I take in her words, the ones I've longed to hear, and it's like a missing puzzle piece falls into place in my heart. She completes me, and I will do anything to make this work. I can feel the weight of her love and devotion as I look into her eyes, giving me the courage I need to finally express how I feel. Silence settles between us, thick tension in the air as those three little words dare to escape.

I take her hands in mine, hoping she doesn't notice my palms sweating from the nerves. "Clara, I want to be with you, no matter the distance," I vow. "I love you, and I know we haven't been together that long, but I believe in us. We can navigate this season apart and find a way to make it work, even if I have to fly back and forth over the pond multiple times a week. I don't care. I'll do anything so we can be together."

"Oh, Delano," she whispers before rising up on her knees, wrapping her arms around my neck, and crashing her lips to mine. Our tongues dance, and with every twirl, I get more lost in her, happily drowning in her gentle touch, her sweet smell, her addicting taste. She sucks my bottom lip between her teeth, making my whole body hum with need. As she pulls back, she gently places her hands on my chest, giving me those big, brown doe eyes.

"I love you *so* much," she whispers softly.

I never knew how much I was missing before Clara. I had sworn off love, thinking all I needed was my ambition. I was so painfully wrong.

"I don't want to go back to New York, but I think I have to, at least for the Spring Season. Then I can see if the London Ballet will be willing to extend my offer."

"I know, baby. It's going to be hard, but we will get through it," I tell her as I pull her down on top of me. I love looking up at her like this, her golden hair a halo around this sweet angel of a human I somehow got lucky enough to call mine.

"Tell me you're mine," I demand.

"I'm yours, and you're mine," she tells me ever so sweetly. We spend the rest of the morning tangled in my sheets, showing each other just how much we truly do belong to each other, body, heart, and soul.

Grand Finale

Clara

In the days that follow, we soak up every moment we have together between my Nutcracker performances. We stroll through London's enchanting streets, hand in hand, enjoying the holiday spirit as much as possible, despite my looming departure.

I've found I'm completely obsessed with the Christmas markets, and Delano patiently walks the cute stalls with me as I pick out presents for my parents. Each evening, we come home and ravish each other in and out of bed, multiple times. Delano plays my body like a violin–I had no idea sex could be so incredible until I met him. He's had me every which way, and I've never been more thankful for my flexibility. It's like my impending departure has us feverish for each other, trying to grasp onto each other as much as possible.

My move back to New York weighs heavily on us both, no matter how many plans we have to be reunited as soon as possible. I hate to leave him right before Christmas, but rehearsals for Swan Lake start the day after.

As thrilled as I should be to finally perform the lead role of Odette after so many years as a baby swan, it's overshadowed by the fact that it will be with ABC and not the London Ballet. When I explained what happened to Madame Ginger, she was completely understanding and assured me that my place with them was secure for next season. Both Delano and I were so incredibly relieved, and it helped us both to feel a bit less anxious about the future.

As the day of my departure arrived, we forced ourselves to cling to the hope that we'd see each other soon. Delano insisted I take his private plane back to New York, and who was I to say no? My partner Trevor and his husband joined me, and I was thankful for the company to distract me from the tears threatening to erupt out of me.

I stand before Delano on the plane's ramp, our eyes locked in a mixture of love and sadness.

"Come back to me, my Sugarplum," he says as he kisses my knuckles. We made plans for me to fly back here on New Year's Day. Sadly, I have rehearsals the morning of New Year's Eve, and he has business meetings that couldn't be re-arranged so that we could celebrate together, but I'm sure we'll make it up to each other the day after.

"Happily," I say before kissing and hugging him one last time. "I love you. Thank you for everything. These have been the best, most magical months of my life."

He tells me he loves me more, and I inhale his scent deeply before pulling away. I refuse to say goodbye, so instead, I turn around and board the plane back to New York with a heavy heart. Once I'm seated, I look out the little window to find Delano still standing, his eyes never leaving mine until the very last moment.

As the plane takes off, carrying me across the vast expanse of the Atlantic, I can't shake the wrongness of leaving him. All I can do is hold onto the belief that Delano and I will survive the next couple of weeks until we're back in each other's arms.

***

I used to think my life would feel complete once I became a principal dancer, but instead, I'm miserable. I'm merely going through the motions: wake up, drink coffee, stretch, eat, ballet class, rehearsals, go home, take a bath, go to sleep. New York, which once felt vibrant and full of promise, now seems lacking, as if a piece of my heart has been left behind in London. The joy I once felt now feels muted, overshadowed by the void left by Delano's absence.

My only reprieve is when I text, call, or video chat with Delano. Those moments get me through my day. The ache of missing him pervades all my thoughts. I long for the comfort of his presence, the warmth of his embrace, the ease of being together. My mind constantly drifts to memories of our time together; the way he holds my hand, the sound of his laughter, the tender moments we shared.

New York isn't home anymore. Delano swept into my life, whisked me away to London, saving me from Mark, and in a couple months, he became my home.

Thankfully, Mark has kept his distance since I returned. I have a feeling Delano issued more threats to ensure that was the case. Gabby also seems to be keeping a close eye out, helping make sure I'm never alone when we're in the studio. She's been the one good thing about being back in New York. She even came home to spend Christmas with my family, since our rehearsals started the next day. It was fun to have some girl time and gush about Delano. She keeps teasing me, calling him my prince. I'm so glad she's happy for me and approves, despite the fact that I will be leaving her behind yet again.

The week after Christmas flies by because I was so busy rehearsing, and now, it's New Year's Eve, and I cannot wait to fly back to London tomorrow. Still, I'm trying to be mindful of the present and enjoy ringing in the new year with Gabby. She insisted we get all fancy tonight and go out to one of our favorite rooftop bars, despite it being freezing and me having an early morning flight.

It's almost midnight, and I'm sipping champagne while Gabby chats away with some guy she found to be her new year's kiss. Watching them flirt is cute, but it makes me miss Delano so much. Thoughts of him consume me, his absence a palpable ache within my soul.

Just as the jubilant crowd starts counting down, I feel a tap on my shoulder. I turn, my eyes widening in astonishment when I see Delano standing before me, a warm smile illuminating his handsome face.

"Delano?" I gasp, my voice filled with a mixture of surprise and joy. "What are you doing here?"

Delano takes my hands in his, his gaze filled with unwavering determination. "I couldn't bear the thought of not kissing you at midnight," he says, his voice filled with longing.

"Five, four, three, two, one... Happy New Year!" the crowd shouts around us as Auld Lang Syne plays through the speakers.

"Happy New Year, Clara," he murmurs as he threads his hands through my hair, pulling me into him as our mouths meet for the first time in two weeks. We kiss each other deeply, groaning into each other's mouths, and God, how I've missed this. Missed *him*. He pulls back slowly, cupping my face with both hands, looking at me like I'm the sun he orbits around. "I want to do whatever it takes to make this work, to be together. I can't stand being away from you. I'm willing to move my headquarters to New York if that's what it takes. I want us to build a life together."

My heart swells with emotions, eyes shimmering with tears of happiness. I've been feeling the same exact way.

"Delano," I whisper, my voice quivering with a mixture of love and vulnerability. "I... I'm not happy dancing for the American Ballet Company. My heart belongs in London with you. I haven't signed my contract yet, and I'm not going to. I want to go home. Take me home." Delano's eyes widen, his surprise mingling with pride.

As the confetti rains down around us, Delano drops to one knee, his eyes locked with mine. My mouth drops open at the realization of what's about to happen. From his pocket, he pulls out a glistening diamond ring, and a gasp escapes me as I cover my mouth in shock.

"Clara, I've never loved anyone like I love you. You say I saved you, but in so many ways, you've saved me. I was a lonely bastard before you, but with you, I feel like I'm whole again," he says, his voice filled with hope and adoration. "Will you marry me? Will you make me the happiest man and do me the honor of being my wife?"

Tears cascade down my cheeks as I nod, and I watch as Delano carefully slides the ring on my finger before pulling me into a hug and kissing every inch of my face. I'm pulled out of our little bubble by Gabby, who crushes me with a hug, squealing congratulations.

At that moment, as a new year begins and our love story starts its second act, I have never been more thankful that Delano saved his Sugarplum.

THE END

Bonus Scene

Want to see what Clara and Delano are up to five years from now?

Go to: https://BookHip.com/NMWXKPS to get the free bonus scene!

Acknowledgements

Thank you so much for reading Saving Sugarplum! This book was such a joy for me to write because of growing up as a ballerina. To turn my childhood dreams into an adult fantasy was beyond fun. I can't wait to write the next book in the Ballerinas and Billionaires series, so stay tuned!

I would first like to thank all of the bookstagrammers and booktokers for showing Saving Sugarplum so much love. Without you sharing my posts and making your own to promote my books, this wouldn't be possible.

A huge thank you to my Street Team! I love you all so much and am so grateful for your support! You make writing and releasing books so much more enjoyable with how you hype me up!

Thank you Jenessa for being such a quality alpha reader and a wonderful friend! Without your feedback and encouragement, I'm not sure where this book would be!

Thank you to my editor Alexa. You are simply the best and I'm so excited to keep working together.

To my parents, thank you for all the years of ballet lessons and Nutcracker seasons, for being at every performance and supporting my passion for dance. It was the most magical childhood.

To my husband and sons, thank you for giving me the time to write and for being my biggest fans.

About the Author

Michelle Moras is a romantic at heart and a lover of all things magical and mythical. Her love of mythology and folklore started over a decade ago while earning her BA degree in History. Ballet was her first love, so it's no surprise her novels have similar themes. When Michelle is not reading and writing, she loves to take naps, drink wine, and dream up her next book plot.

Follow Michelle on her instagram @michellemorasauthor